THE STORY OF A SMALL TOWN LIBRARY

THE STORY OF
A SMALL TOWN LIBRARY

The Development of the Woodstock, N. Y., Library

FRANCES ROGERS

With an Introduction and Notes by
ALF EVERS

THE OVERLOOK PRESS

Woodstock, New York

First published in 1974 by
The Overlook Press
Lewis Hollow Road
Woodstock, New York 12498

Copyright © 1974 by The Woodstock Library
Library of Congress Catalog Card Number: 73-87135
SBN: 0-87951-019-6

Printed in the United States of America
Second printing

To
the men and women who have
donated time and energy to
the making of the
Woodstock Library

Contents

Contents

Introduction

In her history of the Woodstock, N.Y., Library from its beginning in 1913 to the present, Frances Rogers has written a lively narrative which, like all good local history, relates its subject to its background of community life. That is why it seems appropriate to me to use the space allotted for an introduction to outline the library's background in pre-1913 Woodstock. No library freely open to the public existed there, yet the circulation of books was by no means unknown.

The story of Woodstock before the arrival of its art colony in 1902 does not conform to the usual myths of American history. Until the 1850's most of the town's land was held by rich absentee landlords; much of it was occupied after settlement began in 1762 on Old World leases for three lives with rents paid in bushels of wheat, "fat hens," and days of labor. Following the death of the last of the three persons named in the lease, the land would return to its landlord. The Livingstons of the great estate of Clermont, opposite Saugerties on the Hudson River and about twelve miles to the east of Woodstock, were the chief Woodstock landlords. The Livingstons were cultured people who were proud of their fine private library — it was, of course, inaccessible to their tenants. But by 1795 Woodstock people had the right to use the library set up at the Kingston Academy at the expense of the State Board of Regents. A book cost only fourpence per week, but Woodstock tenants did not take advantage of this opportunity because few of them could read. Most of them signed their leases with an "X."

The opening of the Kingston Academy library and legislative acts aimed at creating a system of elementary schools for the State reflected a conviction that the people of a democracy must be able to read and must have access to information by means of print. By 1797 a schoolhouse was standing in Woodstock. Classes were held irregularly until 1815 when a town-wide system of seven district schools was set up under recent acts of the legislature. In 1835 the legislature provided partial funds for establishing libraries in the State's district schools. In 1845 Dr. Stephen L. Heath, as Woodstock's Commissioner of Schools, reported spending $76.50 that year on books for his town's school libraries.

Once elementary schools had begun to function, a rapid increase in literacy followed among both men and women. Books had not been listed in inventories of early Woodstock estates; by the 1830's books on such subjects as midwifery, horse doctoring, farming methods, religion, and the lives of American heroes were being bought and read in Woodstock. And a new kind of library was coming to town.

The new kind of library was a Sunday school library and by the time of the Civil War such libraries had grown to formidable size, existed throughout much of the United States, and were exerting a strong influence on American life. The books they offered had little in common with the lives of great men, the histories, and the abridged versions of the classics on the shelves of the school district libraries. They specialized instead in attractively printed and illustrated little tales designed to give an often heavy-handed religious or moral lesson. At the same time the changing of Woodstock into a summer resort for city dwellers was resulting in the installation in hotels and boarding-houses of collections of very miscellaneous books which boarders might use on rainy days and which neighbors might borrow during the dull days of winter.

The Sunday School libraries reached their peak during the 1870's and then declined under widespread criticism of the namby-pamby quality of most of their books. But by then the work of the common school system had produced in Woodstock as elsewhere a generation of readers who demanded something better than the newspapers and limited collections of books to which they had easy access. By the 1880's state legislatures were taking action to make possible in almost every sizeable American town a free library, jointly funded by state and town. Existing libraries which were owned by clubs for the use of their members were urged to enlarge their usefulness by going public. New York State Librarian Melvil Dewey, greatest of innovators in American library methods, worked at devising programs for converting school district libraries into free public libraries, for sending circulating collections of books into the State's small towns, and for encouraging people throughout the State to organize local libraries with the help available under new laws.

The earliest attempts at bringing libraries to the region of the Catskills had taken the form of what were known as "society libraries." An example was the projected library of the Durham Company in Greene County in 1793. Shareholders in libraries like this were entitled to borrow books usually upon paying an annual fee. As the Catskills developed into a summer resort region, many small membership libraries appeared. By the 1890's discussions about organizing libraries were going on in every resort town in the region. In Fleischmanns and Pine Hill impressively housed libraries were endowed as memorials to members of wealthy summer families. The exclusive Onteora Club at Tannersville set up a library for its members. In Roxbury the society library which had been in business between 1816 and 1835 was revived with financial backing from Helen Gould, daughter of the town's multi-millionaire Jay Gould; in 1903 it became a free public library.

Through the 1890's and the early years of the twentieth century Woodstock people talked about joining to found a library but no concrete results followed. Nor did any summer visitor offer to build a memorial library. In 1903 Ralph Radcliffe Whitehead installed his own library, rich in books on art, the crafts, music, and literature, in a room adjoining the school of art which opened that year at his colony of Byrdcliffe. The Whitehead library was open not to the general public but only to the art students and craftsmen of Byrdcliffe. Then, in 1913, Whitehead took the lead in bringing a library to a wider Woodstock public. How he helped organize the Woodstock Club and how the Club evolved into the town's present library is the subject of the pages that follow. And thanks to Frances Rogers' painstaking care in research and skill in writing, this account of the evolution of a library becomes a fascinating contribution to an understanding of small-town American life.

ALF EVERS

PART ONE : 1902-1927

1

The Village and the Arts and Crafts Colony

While the story of the Woodstock Library parallels that of many other small-town libraries in a number of ways, there are some particular features in the history of the town of Woodstock — in its cultural, political, social development — that have given certain unique twists and turns to its growth, and that have indelibly marked its character. So it is well, first of all, to review the nature of the village, the society in which the Library found its roots and in which it grew.

In the early 1900's Woodstock in the Catskills was a small horse-and-buggy village, and except for the growing arts and crafts colony, well up on the southern slope of Overlook Mountain, very little in the long established settlement seemed likely to change. There was no library, no place where one could sit and read, or better still, borrow books to carry home: and if one can judge from the attitude of the Town Board when put to the test, the village would have gone without a library of any kind for a very long time indeed — but for the Woodstock Club.

The Woodstock Club? It was one of the twists and turns along the way which we will come to presently.

As for the village itself, during the summer season quite a number of the local people made a practice of taking in "paying guests." These visitors would stay a while then leave without causing so much as a ripple in the everyday life of the place. Doubtless far more vacationers would have gladly spent a few days in the beautiful valley if Woodstock had not been so difficult to reach.

From New York the journey began by ferry across the

Hudson River to board a train in Weehawken on the Jersey side. Kingston was a scant hundred miles upstate, but it was a long, sooty ride with frequent stops at small stations. Upon reaching Kingston those bound for Woodstock waited in the railway station for the local train which would carry them at what seemed little better than a snail's pace up the long steep grade to West Hurley, a sparsely settled hamlet. The last leg of the trip was made in an open bus drawn by a pair of gray horses. It was six or seven miles of uneven country road up hill and down. Then, at long last, Woodstock.

Summer boarders would continue to come and go but the village would see few tourists until after the almost unheard of "horseless carriage" had acquired a windshield in 1910 and evolved into the motor car.[1]

What proved to be the opening wedge in the comfortable isolation of the country village was the establishment of Mr. Whitehead's art colony, and the man directly responsible for having selected the site where the colony would be located was Bolton Brown.

Brown had never laid eyes on Ralph Radcliffe Whitehead before the day the wealthy Englishman had called on him at his home in Palo Alto, California. Nor did he know why he, a stranger, was considered the right man to carry out a mission so dear to Whitehead's heart. It had long been Whitehead's dream to found a colony where creative people could work while living a simple and satisfying life. And what he wanted Brown to do was to find the right location

1. Woodstock had been given a big boost as a summer resort by the opening of the Brinkerhoff House in 1869 and the Overlook Mountain House in 1872 — and the word spread when in 1873 President Grant spent a night at the hotel on Overlook. By the early 1880's a number of large farm boarding houses were in operation in Woodstock and almost every farmer was taking care of at least a few summer people. Access to the town was pleasanter during this period than it was to become after 1900. Train service was better and many boarders travelled from New York as far as Kingston or Saugerties on the luxurious Hudson River steamers. [A.E.]

in the country not far from a large city and not less than fifteen hundred feet above sea level.[2]

For Brown, who was a professor of art at Stanford University at the time, it would mean resigning from the University and going on what could readily turn out to be a wild goose chase. Nevertheless, the idea appealed. But when Whitehead said that Asheville, North Carolina, was the vicinity he had in mind, Brown protested. He considered New York preferable to other cities in the east, and since the Catskills were within easy range of that city, he pointed out, there should be no difficulty in finding land high enough to meet specifications.

After they had reached an agreement on the salary Brown would receive, Whitehead said that while Brown was looking for a place in the Catskills, he and his young friend, Hervey White, would go south to see what they could find. "We'll keep in touch," he told Brown, "and decide on our location later."

No papers were signed. Yet Brown was still willing to chance it, to burn his bridges behind him, as it were. He sold his Palo Alto property, packed his belongings, and, accompanied by his wife Lucy and their three babies, traveled east by train to his ancestral home in Schuyler County, N.Y.

"As the crow flies, the Catskills are only some twenty-five miles across," Brown wrote in 1937, "but I used up three entirely laborious weeks zig-zagging back and forth and up and down in them. . . ."

The zig-zagging ended the day he climbed the northern

2. Ralph Radcliffe Whitehead, 1854–1929, was a member of a prosperous family which had been active for generations in the woolens industry of the West Riding of Yorkshire, England. He studied at Harrow and at Balliol College, Oxford, where he came under the influence of social reformer and authority on aesthetics, John Ruskin. Whitehead explained his hopes for founding an essentially Ruskinian arts and crafts colony in *Grass of the Desert*, London, 1892. The following year he emigrated to the United States and settled in Santa Barbara, California, where he wrote and published pamphlets, tried to improve the quality of education in the public schools, and made plans for the colony which came into being in Woodstock, N.Y., in 1902. [A.E.]

slope of Overlook and found himself at Mead's Mountain House. The panoramic view from there was so beautiful it made him catch his breath. In the distance the silvery Hudson gleamed like a metallic thread; below in the valley was a village. "That's Woodstock village," old Mr. Mead told him.

That same afternoon, by tramping across lots, Brown found what he had been searching for: the ideal place for Whitehead's experiment.

In response to a wire from Brown, Whitehead and Hervey White met him in Washington, D.C., and from there the three traveled north together. In Kingston a surrey was hired for the long drive to Mead's Mountain House, and while passing through Woodstock the rig and its occupants did not go unnoticed. Whitehead, a smallish, sandy-haired man with a neat mustache, was fashionably clad in white flannels; Hervey White, bearded, hatless, was wearing a bright red windsor tie.

The tract of farmland for which Brown, after considerable dickering, managed to obtain options, embraced several holdings and amounted to more than twelve hundred acres. Whitehead had not only liked the place but had gone so far as to choose the site where his own house would stand and to name it "White Pines."

By October work on the first of the many studios, workshops, and cottages that would form the nucleus of the arts and crafts colony was well under way. Meanwhile, Brown, his wife Lucy, and the three children were boarding at Ella Riseley's on the Rock City road, just below the corners where that road crossed the Glasco Turnpike. From the first, Lucy and Ella got along famously and it was from Lucy that Ella (and subsequently the whole village) learned why Mr. Whitehead's colony would be known as Byrdcliffe. His wife's middle name was Byrd and by combining it with the last part of his own middle name he had arrived at Byrdcliffe.

In February of 1903 the Browns moved into their new home on the side of the very steep hill. It was five below zero and beginning to snow. Lucy said the air was so cold she could scarcely breathe.

During the winter there had been intermittent visits from Mr. Whitehead who liked to keep an eye on how things were going. And by the time the weather had warmed up, "White Pines" was ready for him, his wife, and two small sons. Much remained to be finished, however, so work continued on the "Viletta," or inn, the large dance hall, and several studios and workshops.

Even before the last of the carpenters had left, friends of the Whiteheads who were interested in his "experiment" arrived to see what Byrdcliffe was like. The Birge Harrisons were among the first visitors, and they were enchanted with the place.[3] They eventually bought adjacent land and built what Brown called an "imposing residence." Next to arrive was the Swedish-born painter, Carl Eric Lindin. He settled in with Hervey White who was camping in an old disused Lutheran church in a pine grove near the village. When Hervey moved to Byrdcliffe, Lindin bought the church and the surrounding land, he said, "right down to the center of the earth for four hundred dollars."

What did the villagers think of this invasion by outsiders? It was hard to tell. When Mr. Whitehead had tried to engage some of them in conversation, they were friendly enough but had almost nothing to say beyond answering his questions. And he himself had great difficulty in overcoming his instinctive reserve.

Almost the only people who took an active interest in

3. (Lovell) Birge Harrison, N.A., 1854–1929, was a well known-landscape painter who became a friend of Ralph Whitehead in Santa Barbara during the 1890's. In 1903 he became director of Whitehead's Byrdcliffe Summer School of Painting. He left at the end of the school's 1904 season and headed the Summer School of the Art Students League of New York established in 1905 at Lyme, Connecticut. In 1906 this school moved to Woodstock with Harrison remaining in Charge. [A.E.]

Byrdcliffe were two individuals who were themselves originally outsiders: Dr. Mortimer Downer and his wife Lillian. The doctor found his now-and-then visits to the mountainside colony of more than passing interest. Lucy Brown in particular took pains to draw him out: she encouraged him to talk about the books he enjoyed reading (history) and his large collection of rare stamps. The day she questioned him about how he, a city man, happened to settle in Woodstock, he told her the whole story, beginning with his student days.

He had married Lillian in 1893, while still an undergraduate at Columbia College of Physicians and Surgeons. Upon earning his M.D. degree he began his practice in Brooklyn, but from the first it was tough going. They had very little money. Then, just when things were looking pretty grim, the unexpected happened. He met a Doctor Smith who said he was from Woodstock.

"I don't remember why he was planning to leave: wanted to better himself, I guess. But I'll never forget the way I jumped at his offer to take me back with him next day so I could see what the place was like and if I wanted to take over his practice when he left." After a short pause the doctor continued: "You should have seen the expression on my wife's face when she opened the box I'd brought back with me. A hundred eggs. I'd paid ten cents a dozen for them.

"We moved up that same year — 1898 — and stayed with the Smiths until our furniture came . . . and it did take some time for a city doctor to get used to a completely new way of life. I got lost more than once, driving back roads at night when it was so dark you couldn't see your hand before your face. But Lillian was a big help. She'd go with me, especially when it was a confinement case. We've made out all right. I love the place and so do my three kids."

What the doctor did not mention was the part he and his wife had played in the life of the community right from the start. Shortly after their arrival he was the one who had stirred up interest in replacing the old stone schoolhouse with a new and far better building. And from then on he had backed every project that would contribute to the civic growth of the village.

In Byrdcliffe, at the end of the first year, Mr. Whitehead did not renew Brown's contract. He was "fired," some said, "because he had not been satisfied with being an obedient employee." Be that as it may, it is known that Brown, who had been in charge of the Drawing and Painting Department at Stanford, had expected to become head of the Byrdcliffe School of Art, and when Birge Harrison was appointed, with Brown as drawing instructor, it may have rankled. Undaunted, Brown purchased land from Ella Riseley and built the house he and his family would occupy for a number of years.

Despite minor problems, the arts and crafts colony appeared to be thriving. There were so many students, in addition to the musicians, craftsmen, and artists, that classes were being held in the dance hall. Yet, after only one year as head of the art school, Birge Harrison resigned. "Papa Whitehead," as he was secretly called, was sorely puzzled. Nor could he understand why so many of the painters objected to knocking off in mid-afternoon, while the light was still good, to take part in the festivities planned by his wife. Artists, he said, were the only people in the world worth living with, and the *most difficult.*

2

The Landscape School of Art; The Maverick and its Concerts and Festivals

In 1906 Woodstock experienced another invasion of outsiders, for that was the year in which Birge Harrison became the chief organizer and instructor of the Landscape School of Art of the Art Students League of New York.[4] A fine old barn had been rented and the upper floor of what had formerly been a livery stable had been converted into a classroom with a big north light and plenty of easels and stools. Located on the site where, some years later, the Tannery Brook House would stand, it was within easy walking distance of several boarding houses. Students could count on getting a room and good country food for seven or eight dollars a week.

On the whole they were a well behaved lot. The small French berets worn by the men served as a trademark (local boys never wore such "silly" things). As for the girls, they dressed according to the fashion of the day when a female's legs were still "limbs": an ankle-length skirt; a shirtwaist with standing collar; and high leather shoes. No young lady would dream of appearing in pants. The word "slacks" did not even exist.

It must be admitted, however, that certain of the farmers

4. As the League opened its Woodstock school, the country was reading newspaper accounts of the raid by Anthony Comstock of the New York Society for the Suppression of Vice on the New York quarters of the League. Comstock seized stocks of the school catalogue and claimed that it contained obscene pictures — some were drawings of the nude by students who were enrolled at Woodstock. This caused the first of many upsurges in Woodstock of an attitude that associated artists with nudity and immorality, and that was to create much misunderstanding and bitterness over many years. [A.E.]

did object to having their fields used as outdoor classrooms. One of them posted his land with "No Trespassing" signs. He claimed that the day after the class set up easels in his lower pasture, he'd lost his best cow and he was pretty certain she'd swallowed "one of them painty rags they was always leaving behind."

There is no record of how Whitehead felt when Hervey White, who was living in the Lark's Nest, a farmhouse on the Byrdcliffe property, decided to start an arts and crafts colony of his own.[5] He had always been a poor man but an uninhibited one. Actually, Hervey had to borrow a thousand dollars to gain title to the large tract of land, approximately two and a half miles southwest of Woodstock, just over the Hurley boundary line. Being very much of an individualist, he decided to call his new place the "Maverick."

The first musician to become a member of the Maverick group was the cellist, Paul Kefer. He left Byrdcliffe along with his friend Hervey; and it was Kefer who brought an even more distinguished cellist, Horace Britt, into the group. Rather like a chain reaction, Britt, in turn, persuaded the concert master of New York's Metropolitan Opera Orchestra, Pierre Henrotte, that the Maverick was the right place for him. And so it went, with many other fine musicians arriving "to look things over" and then deciding to stay.

Shortly after the start of World War I in 1914, the first real concert by Maverick musicians was held in Firemen's Hall for the benefit of the "starving Belgians." Encouraged by the enthusiastic response to music by professionals, Hervey built the Maverick Music Hall, and when this rustic structure was completed in 1916, there began a series of Sunday Concerts

5. Hervey White, 1866–1944, was a novelist, poet, and social worker. At Woodstock, White had managed the Byrdcliffe farm and the Lark's Nest, to which he invited his many friends in the worlds of art, literature, and social protest. If Whitehead liked a guest at the Lark's Nest, he would invite him to join the Byrdcliffe experiment. [A.E.]

destined to continue without a break for more than half a century.

All was not a bed of roses for Hervey and his "poor man's Byrdcliffe," however. Faced with the need to supply a group of his houses with water, he engaged a team of well-drillers and for many days thereafter the rhythmic pounding, characteristic of a driven well, was heard throughout the Maverick. And when that sound is heard for a long time it is a sure sign that the well is going to be unusually deep. And so it was in this case: water at fifteen hundred forty-four feet at a dollar a foot — a bill Hervey could not pay.

Luckily he had friends inventive enough to think of a way out of the dilemma. They helped him convert his large bluestone quarry into an outdoor theater, complete with stage and tiers of seats. What would become renowned as the First Maverick Festival (1914) was so successful that the gate receipts went a long way toward wiping out that particular debt.

Moreover, the idea caught on, and every August during many summers to come a merry-making, picnic-type festival was held in the big field beyond the Music Hall. And since the entrance fee was double for those who arrived in everyday clothes, almost everyone came in costume of one kind or another. At dusk the field was dotted with campfires; the air was fragrant with the mouth-watering smell of cookout suppers; and at night laughter and group-singing drowned out the chirping of crickets and the rasp of katydids.

During the prohibition era when bathtub gin and other synthetic drinks were being consumed freely, an element alien to the early festivals crept in and gained a foothold. Rather than let rowdiness take over, Hervey White, in 1931, canceled the Maverick Festivals.

3

The Walter Weyls; A New Plan in the Making

One member of his colony whom Whitehead had been particularly pleased to welcome was Louise Starr, a quiet, rather shy young woman from Chicago. She had been teaching bookbinding at Jane Addams' Hull House and now she was looking forward to working on her own. Highly skilled, she "belonged" in Byrdcliffe.

In September of 1907, the house that had been occupied by Hervey White was rented to friends of Louise Starr: Mr. and Mrs. Weyl of Chicago. Walter Weyl and his bride Bertha Poole found the Lark's Nest much to their liking. It was not too far from New York, the hub of the publishing world, a matter of prime importance for a free-lance writer who expected to make a living with his pen.

Louise and young "B. P.," as Bertha was known to her associates at Hull House, had met when she first became involved in settlement work. She was the daughter of a wealthy Chicago family and when she became engaged to the thirty-four-year old Walter Weyl, the Pooles did their best to make their aristocratic, fine-looking daughter "listen to reason." All her life she had been accustomed to the best that money could buy, while Walter, a writer of articles for popular magazines, took pride in his "proven ability to live comfortably on seven dollars a week." Even the threat of disinheritance made no impression on her. Walter was a handsome man, slender and of average height, with strong aquiline features set off by a small moustache and dark goatee. He was warm, outgoing, and witty. Finally the Pooles relented sufficiently to provide an elaborate wedding but that was as far as they were willing to go.

The Weyls had no difficulty in adjusting to a new way of life. Marriage had a galvanizing effect on Walter Weyl's literary output: he was soon earning a good income and a name for himself as well. Then in 1911 the Pooles, having undergone a change of heart, set up a generous trust fund for their daughter, whereupon the Weyls purchased farmland on the side of Ohayo Mountain, across the valley from Overlook. The following year they built a large impressive house and Byrdcliffe lost two more of its distinguished members. It had already lost another couple when Carl Lindin and Louise Starr had married. Together the Lindins remodeled the old church in the pine grove that Carl owned and converted it into a lovely home.

Some years later, when writing about Ralph Radcliffe Whitehead, Hervey White said that Whitehead "could not, he would not adjust himself to the fashions of the times. And the fashions of Art change like all others."

That may account, at least to a minor degree, for the gradual disintegration of the Byrdcliffe arts and crafts colony on the mountainside. One by one those who carved wood, wove rugs, made pottery, or painted on canvas had moved away to settle elsewhere, frequently in the vicinity of Woodstock. But rather than dwell on his disappointment, Whitehead now began to think about and plan a civic program of a very different nature, a project that "the villagers and the rest of us, the outsiders, could share."

By the late summer of 1913 he was ready to discuss his idea with the Lindins, the Downers, and the Weyls. Walter Weyl and his wife Bertha arrived at White Pines in their new car, one of the first in Woodstock. They had gone out of their way to pick up the Lindins and by the time they reached White Pines the overheated radiator was spouting steam. The high, spidery-looking "touring car" had a top that could be folded back and side curtains, with isinglass windows, to be snapped on when it rained.

Weyl, who was always on the lookout for new "projects," expressed wholehearted approval. He said he believed that "even a mere magazine writer could be a man of enormous influence in the community," and he could think of nothing that would be of greater value to the town than a library, even a small one.

Dr. Downer agreed but felt that there should be a health program of some kind, possibly one that included engaging a trained nurse who could serve in case of need.

After a spirited discussion about ways in which to raise funds, a decision was reached: the first step would be the selection of a group of charter members for the new Woodstock Club. They were to be a cross-section of the community, a group capable of planning details such as arranging for an open meeting and staging a drive for membership.

4

The Woodstock Club and its Fledgling Library

The first open meeting of the newly organized Club was held on November 12 in Firemen's Hall. Everyone had been urged to attend and learn firsthand what the founders hoped to accomplish and what plans were in the making.

The hall was one of the landmarks of the village. Out front hung the huge iron ring that served as a fire alarm. When struck with the accompanying hammer the noisy clanging brought the volunteer firemen on the run. Inside, near the entrance, stood the only fire-fighting equipment for miles around: a large, red, hand-pulled, hand-pumped fire engine and a two-wheeled hose cart.

By eight o'clock that chill Wednesday evening all but a few of the folding chairs were taken. The artists had turned out in full force and the villagers, too, were well represented. Seated on the raised platform at the end of the long hall were three of the charter members of the Club: Mr. Whitehead, Mr. Weyl, and Dr. Downer, the chairman. And when the latter rose to speak all coughing ceased abruptly.

After expressing his pleasure at seeing so many familiar faces in the audience, Dr. Downer introduced the first speaker, Mr. Whitehead, who would, he said, "explain the objectives of the Woodstock Club."

From the Club's minutes, written more than half a century ago, much may be learned about how the meeting was conducted, but the secretary did not include even a brief summary of what either speaker said. It is safe to assume, however, that it was Mr. Whitehead who enlarged on a plan to set up a nurse's fund that would be used, in cases of need, to engage a trained nurse. That probably brought a round of applause. Walter Weyl, always an entertaining speaker with his skill for holding the attention of an audience with witty side remarks, must have stressed what he himself firmly believed: even a small town should have a library because, in order to lead a full life, its people must have access to far more books than they themselves could afford to buy.

The reaction to what Mr. Weyl said was polite, but it was his reply to a question from the floor that was greeted with instant enthusiasm.

"You ask how the Club expects to raise the money for the nurse's fund," he said. "Well, my friend, I will tell you. Plans are already under way for the Club to buy a motion picture projector and hold picture shows once or twice a week here in Firemen's Hall."

There was spontaneous applause. Movies were the least expensive and most popular form of entertainment, for this was well before the early days of radio broadcasting. And the trip to Kingston to see a movie meant a two-hour drive each way.

The Club did have other plans up its sleeve, one being that if enough people joined at a dollar or more a year, the dues alone would provide a good income. According to the minutes, George Elwyn and Harry Brink (both local men) were appointed by the chair to list the names of those present who were willing to become members. But the secretary (whoever he was) must have become so interested in what followed (who signed up, who didn't) that he failed to keep track of the count. The entry reads: "These names added to those already promised make a total of   .

A tantalizing blank that never was filled in.

He did note, however, that a committee of five was appointed to draw up the Constitution and Bye-laws (*sic*) for the Club and report at the next meeting.

Based on Robert's *Rules of Order,* the bylaws drafted by

the committee and presented on Saturday evening, November 15, were in no way unusual except for the final clause: "There shall be no gambling nor shall any alcoholic drinks be consumed on the premises of the Club." Now that so many young students were attending the League's summer school, was it not the Club's duty to anticipate and forestall trouble?

As for the committee appointed "to look for the best premises," nothing could have been simpler. George Neher, a contractor and builder, was so favorably impressed by what the Club could do for Woodstock that he offered to convert the ground floor of a building (actually a barn) he had recently purchased into a large room suitable for its library.

"The rent," he said, "would be only ten dollars a month." Mr. Neher figured that he could make the upper story into a studio. Studios were in short supply and later he had no difficulty at all in finding a tenant — Mrs. Watkins, a painter from Chicago.

Mr. Neher's offer was promptly accepted by the Club. True, the rent would be low, but what was even more important was the location of the building. It was on the State Road not far from the Tannery Brook bridge. There is no record of just when the Club took possession of its new quarters. About all that can be learned from those early minutes is that a coal stove, together with the cost of installing bookshelves and furnishing the room, called for an initial outlay of $40. No money, it seems, had to be spent for books since they could be donated by the members.

The committee in charge of library affairs was headed by Margaret (Mrs. John) Carlson. John had been among the first artists to leave Byrdcliffe in a huff, fed up with restrictions imposed by its founder. Later he had become Birge Harrison's successor at the League. And it was John Carlson who, during a conversation with one of his friends, Marion Eames, had so stirred her interest in Woodstock that she was now making it her home. A young woman with a fine soprano voice and an active interest in civic affairs, Marion told Margaret that she would be glad to serve on the Library Committee. Two others who agreed to "do what they could" were Birge Harrison and Carl Lindin.

As outlined in the minutes, their duties consisted of writing thank-you notes to those who had donated books, ordering coal as needed, and engaging a librarian. Almost any reasonably well-read layman, known to the directors, would be acceptable provided he or she was willing to work for fifty cents an hour. But there is no record as to how many hours, or days a week, the library would be open to the public. Apparently the Club's new secretary, the Rev. Mr. Clough, saw no point in cluttering up the minutes with minor details. He was far more interested in seeing to it that the Club would have nothing to regret. In an entry dated November 25 we find the following: "After considerable discussion on the question of allowing forms of entertainment it was, upon motion, resolved that no dances be held under the auspices of the Club at present."

When the board of directors met again at Dr. Downer's, this time in December, it discussed the long-pending plan to hold motion picture shows in Firemen's Hall. By unanimous vote it was "resolved to purchase for $275 a Simplex Moving Picture machine."

Then comes a gap of nine months. It is like reading a story with half the pages missing. And if it were not for some of the old-timers who attended the Club's early shows we might never have known what went wrong. This, however, is what actually happened: the engine and generator rigged up to supply current for the projector had a way of breaking down at unpredictable intervals, bringing the show to an abrupt halt while one of the men tinkered valiantly with the engine to get it going again. And each time the screen went blank the audience responded with groans and laughter. This occurred so often that it became a bad joke and the Club decided to call the whole thing off and get rid of the projector.

When the Club held its annual members' meeting in September of 1914, the new secretary, Edward Simmons, who had a dairy farm on Van De Bogart hill, was "given authority to sell Moving Picture Machine for $200 and if unable to get that much report to the Board of Directors."

It was at this same meeting that Mrs. Weyl made a motion, which Mr. Whitehead seconded, to spend twenty dollars for new books "at once."

Possibly it was the librarian, Francis Clough, a young man with a taste for poetry, who had informed the board that there had been many requests for books not on the shelves. What the Club's library had been offering its reading public up to this point had been a collection of secondhand books.

The new chairman of the Library Committee, Walter Weyl, welcomed the assignment. At the directors' meeting in November he reported that "$18.50 had been spent for fifty new books." Also that the Committee had decided to put a box in the library "in which people might drop a card with a list of books they would like to read."

The crowning touch, however, was Walter Weyl's offer to try to secure new books from publishers "as nearly free as possible."

How did Mr. Weyl make out? There is no reference to his report in subsequent minutes. We learn that the Club had a balance in the general fund of $106 and $90 in the Nurse's Fund. Also that the resignation of Librarian Francis Clough was "accepted with thanks" and that his successor was a young artist named Richardson Gray.

During the winter several "social meetings" had been held in the library. They cost the Club next to nothing because "Mrs. Weyl had donated coffee, Mr. George Elwyn sugar, and Mr. Edward Simmons cream."

In June the proceeds from a rummage sale amounted to $162 and a benefit concert in August netted $63. Then in

September of 1915 the board of directors really stepped out: a letter was sent to the State Library in Albany requesting information "concerning the change from a private to a public library."

When the reply was received the Club found that there are two kinds of public libraries: one, a library established by the officials of a town or city and supported by the tax-payers; the other, known as an association library, "is established and controlled, in whole or in part, by a group of individuals operating as an association or as trustees" (a group of individuals who could guarantee running expenses, of course).

Unfortunately, the directors of the Woodstock Club could not qualify — they were operating on a shoestring, never quite sure how much longer they could keep their small library going.

If we can judge by the entry in the minutes, the directors expressed no regret. It reads: "It was not deemed advisable by the committee to make the change to a public at the present time."

"Advisable"? Well, that was one way of looking at it.

5

The Club Tries Again

At this same meeting in September the matter of a new engine and generator to be used with the motion picture machine (the one that had not been sold by the secretary) was discussed. And the chairman of the Entertainment Committee reported that the cost of installment in Firemen's Hall, including the fireproof booth that was required by law, would amount to about $450.

Two of those present (unnamed in the minutes) must have considered this a wise investment. They promised a donation of $100 (each?) toward the sum needed "on condition that the rest of the money be raised by October 1st."

Probably that deadline was extended, for at a meeting of the board of directors on October 5, the newly-elected chairman of the Entertainment Committee, Ralph Whitehead, said that it had been decided "to put all efforts in motion picture machine [and] to have a Hallowe'en supper for same."

"All efforts"? There must have been a hitch somewhere even if the committee worked with all deliberate speed. Eight months later, in May 1916, we find the vote "to install a motion picture apparatus" repeated in much the same words. Then in June, Henry Peper, a member of the board of directors, was appointed a committee of one to go to Saugerties and "receive instructions in how to run the machine, and to engage an experienced man for the first performance."

A blacksmith by trade, Mr. Peper could do almost anything with iron. His handwrought hinges, door latches, fire irons, and candlesticks were proudly displayed by those who acquired them. As might be expected, Mr. Peper had no difficulty in following instructions when the man in Saugerties showed him how to thread the film through the projector and how to crank it by hand at just the right pace. In addition he had to learn to cement the broken ends of a film together as quickly as possible. The Club would be getting its films by mail from an agency, films that were far from new and might break two or three times during a show. Many of the movies would be two-reelers; therefore he would have to know how to change reels and rewind them.

At the time Mr. Peper was receiving his instructions, the plan to build a fireproof booth to house the projector did not seem too complicated. But for one reason or another the work dragged on and on and at the Annual Meeting in September 1916 "the Comm. in charge of the work at the Firemen's Hall reported a delay in the electrical work but hope to have the work completed very shortly."

Encouraged by this, the directors voted in October to engage Mr. Peper "to take charge of the Moving Picture Machine at $2.00 per evening." But seven months later, in May 1917, the directors were still discussing what remained to be done before the opening, presumably in June. "Miss Eames," we are told, "promised the donation of an electric drop light for the piano." Before the day that moving pictures learned to speak for themselves, a piano to supply "mood" music for silent movies was considered necessary. "The committee in charge of moving pictures was empowered to have the curtain mounted on rollers and painted, and to buy a suitable step ladder or have steps built up to the booth."

This is the last entry about the Club's movies for two months. Not a word about the opening, but all must have been going well because at the directors' meeting in July the "advisability of two moving picture shows in one week" was discussed. The Club did have other irons in the fire. A bazaar, held the previous year in the Firemen's Hall, had netted the impressive sum of $690 and it was hoped that the one being planned for the summer would do as well because "the Suffrage and Red Cross had been invited to cooperate."

All in all there was good reason to be pleased with the way things were going, and Mrs. Weyl was asked to prepare a leaflet covering the Club's activities during the past four years. This she did so well that the leaflet, entitled "What Does the Woodstock Club Do?" was printed and "mailed to every family in town." Unfortunately, so far as we know, not a single copy can be located, but it did start a trend. Other brochures would be printed and distributed in 1929, 1936, and 1955.

A report neatly typed by the chairman of the Library Committee (Bruce Herrick at the time) and attached by its corners to a page in the book of minutes gives much welcome information. "During the year ending September 1, 1917," it begins, "the interest in the Club library has been such as to encourage those who have the interest of the library at heart and to warrant great hopes for its continued growth and prosperity . . . the number of periodicals recently sub- scribed to has encouraged more and more use of the library as a public reading room.

"It is estimated that during the year of 1917 twenty volumes per day have been taken out or a total for the 312 days of 6240 volumes. It is impossible to state just what per- centage of these were fiction but the librarian reports a con- stant tendency to take from the library shelves books of a more serious nature.

"The total number of books at present in the library is about 1400 which it is the purpose of the Club to add to from time to time.

"About one hundred volumes have recently been added among which are several notable books on the European war and other subjects. . . . All together the library has become a permanent and much appreciated factor in our village life and should continue to grow and increase in interest as Woodstock itself continues to grow."

How well Mr. Herrick foretold the future without the aid of a crystal ball. Yet just ahead lay a difficult period.

6

Closed for the Coming Winter;
The Market Fair

During 1917, only by dint of everyone's hard work was the Club kept going; in November the chairman of the Moving Picture Committee reported that for the past five weeks the shows had been running at a deficit of more than $40 a week. "The nightly expenses are $25 and to cover that," he said, "a full house is required." Even so, the Board decided that "the shows should continue for the present."

It was a decision that seems rather odd considering how little money the Club actually had. The treasurer's report gives a grand total of $555.07 on hand, but a large part of this was tied up in the Nurse Fund and could not be used for running expenses. When Mrs. Martin Schutze had donated $190, the gift had been earmarked for that fund, bringing its total to $244.25, but during the winter $24.36 had been spent for "three cases of illness." After the outstanding bills were paid only $127.84 remained in the general fund. So the board reversed itself. Not only were the picture shows closed for the coming winter but the library, too, was closed "owing to a shortage of coal."

No meetings were held during the winter, but before the beginning of the new season in May of 1918 the Club's early minutes had been copied and the original notes destroyed. This explains why the minutes in *Book One* are typed (probably by Bruce Herrick) on loose leaf pages and clamped together between hard covers while the subsequent minutes in *Book Two* are in longhand throughout. It may also account for the many gaps in the record: when the scribbled notes were too difficult to decipher, the typist skipped them.

In the hope of attracting more young people to the library, a billiard table had been installed in a small room opening off the reading room and George Neher had agreed to take charge of the evening games. It was a good move but those extra hours increased the cost of heating and lighting the library at a time when there was little money to spare.

In June the directors took a long hard look at the treasurer's report and appointed a committee of three — Mr. Whitehead, Mrs. J. A. Murray (a new member), and Mr. Neher — "To see the Town Board and ask their assistance in meeting the expenses of the library." Although the town fathers may have realized that the community owed much to the Club, the petition was refused and the matter was dropped.

There is no record of what happened next; all but two pages of the Club's minutes for 1919 are missing, but the last sentence on one of these refers briefly to "the Market Fair."

For a number of years the Market Fair, started in 1918 as a war project, contributed generously to the Woodstock Club and because the origin of the Fair has been all but forgotten, a short summary of how it began and how it functioned seems in order. In the spring of 1917, Mrs. Orville (Ethel) Peets, with the picturesque street markets of Paris in mind, hit upon the idea of holding a "street market sort of fair" in the center of the village "to raise money for the Red Cross." And among those with whom she discussed the matter was Marion Eames, one of the directors, and she in turn, talked it over with the other members of the Club — not that the Club would in any way be responsible for the venture but in the hope of rounding up volunteer workers.

Ethel Peets herself, with the help of Mrs. Chase (the mother of Rhoda Chase, illustrator) supervised the first of the many Saturday morning fairs held on the village green opposite the Dutch Reformed Church. Everybody gave and everybody bought. All the homemade cakes, pies, and bread, pickles, jellies, homegrown vegetables and flowers were donated. There had never been anything in Woodstock quite like this event, for which so much was given so enthusiastically. And the money rolled in. Held weekly throughout that summer and for many summers thereafter, the Market Fair continued to flourish. Fourteen years after that first fair, *The Woodstock Press* ran an article based on the memory of several old-timers:

Going back to the first year, the older residents who took part in it have many amusing stories to tell. There was the flower table in charge of Mrs. Martin Schutze who practically cleaned out her garden for the Fair. Many others did the same and it took on almost the proportions of a flower show. One day Mrs. Henry Lee McFee came with a great bunch of larkspur and Canterbury Bells — Eugene Speicher at once bought it, took it home and painted the flowers. Mr. and Mrs. Carl Eric Lindin bought the canvas and it now hangs (a very stunning Speicher) on the wall of their dining room.

In the war years the entire profits were given [to the Red Cross]. People gave outright of the thing they could make best and got no return in money. Mrs. McFee's rolls were even more famous than her larkspur and when she came in sight walking down the Rock City road with a basket of fresh rolls on her arm, she would be met a quarter of a mile out by eager purchasers who feared to lose their chance if they waited until she reached the market.

Ethel Peets' flowers and her stuffed eggs were awaited as eagerly. Marion Bullard made sponge cake. Marion Eames often contributed clothing and one customer waited for her shoes, always they were an exact fit and would be carried over to the horse block in front of the church for trying on. All the shoes were fitted there.

Among the most popular articles were bales of paint rags rolled up and tied, bought by art students and contributed from attics and scrap bags all over the village. . . . Mrs. Ned Chase started the vogue for calico neckties made by herself and almost every man in Woodstock was wearing a twenty-five cent necktie made of calico from the Bearsville store.

During the ten years between 1920 and 1930 the sum of $4,478.19 has been disbursed by the managers of the Market Fair. . . . The Women's Club, the Library and the Firemen have been given generous amounts each year — $150, $200 as the receipts permitted. . . .

Many a canvas has been painted of the Market Fair with its striped umbrellas, gay wares, vivid frocks and jackets and visitors to Woodstock carry away with them memory of one of the most delightful sights to be found in any village anywhere. . . .

7

Woodstock's Who's Who in the Arts, and the New Gallery

In November of 1919 came the sobering news from New York that Walter Weyl, the widely known writer, editor, and economist, had died. But in Woodstock, in particular, his name would live on in permanent form, as will be described presently.

The village he had so dearly loved showed few signs of change beyond the number of cars (many of them "tin lizzies") and pickup trucks that traveled its dirt roads. Bicycles were as popular as ever. John Carlson and his wife Margaret were frequently seen peddling about on their "Bicycle Built for Two." She in skirts, of course — the pantsuit was still not so much as a speck on the horizon.

Yet by the 1920's few places in America could claim such an array of talent as this one small valley in the Catskills. And now there was need of a gallery where artists could have their work on exhibition.

In order to finance the construction of a gallery, a group of local artists organized the Woodstock Realty Company. And two years later, in 1922, the completed building, a white Colonial-type structure close to the Village Green, was leased to the newly formed Woodstock Artists Association for its first exhibition. The *New York Times* called it a first rate exhibition, a real movement underway. . . .

Thanks to Carl Eric Lindin's article, published in *The Overlook* in September of 1939, we get a close-up look at a few of the widely known artists.

Of Eugene Speicher, Lindin wrote: "He has great ambitions and has disciplined himself to a difficult task, that is, giving expression to the most worthwhile things in life: feminine beauty, masculine strength, rugged American landscapes and colorful charm of flowers. . . ."

George Bellows, Speicher's neighbor in Rock City, was also summed up well by Lindin when he said that Bellows' whole interest lay in "everyday life, which he painted better than anyone else; whether in his characteristic portraits, or in his descriptions of the tumultuous world which surrounds the prize fighters, or the Bible Sunday revival meetings. . . . In large figure compositions, in hundreds of drawings and lithographs he has illuminated American life."

Lindin then went on to say that he used to watch Henry Lee McFee, who also lived near the Rock City Corners, at work on pictures that grew from "the first careful placing of the composition on the canvas to those last deliberate touches which make the complete masterpiece."

Space does not allow listing more than a few of the other notable members of the Woodstock Artists Association: Konrad Cramer, Alfeo Faggi, Ernest Fiene, Emil Ganso, Norbert Heermann, Alfred Hutty, Neil Ives, Kaj and Georgina Klitgaard, Paul and Caroline Rohland, Yasuo Kuniyoshi, Henry Mattson, Charles Rosen, Judson Smith, Carl Walters, Herminie Kleinert, Arnold Wiltz, are some of the many distinguished names.

These artists as well as numerous others contributed generously to the growing Woodstock Library. Some of them helped build what would become its unique collection of art books; others donated drawings to be raffled off on Fair Day; while still others served as salesmen at one of the booths or tables.

But for these artists the Woodstock Library might have been more like other small-town libraries.

8

New Quarters for the Library;
Again the Town Board Turns a Deaf Ear

In 1920, at the close of the summer season, the Club received a check for $300 from the Market Fair, a contribution greatly appreciated. Even so, there was pressing need for enough money to keep the Club going and at the October meeting of the board of directors there was a discussion regarding "the advisability of the Club's co-operating with the Town Board with a view to maintain the library together." Those not in favor of such a step argued that if the town fathers had refused in 1918 to contribute even a small sum to the upkeep of the library, how could they be expected to co-operate in "maintaining" it? "After further discussion," the secretary wrote, "the plan was dismissed as inadvisable."

The following spring those in charge of motion pictures welcomed a change in management: they turned the operation of the shows over to professionals and signed a contract with the McClean brothers of Kingston, who had agreed to rent the entire outfit for "$7.00 a night for twenty-five or more shows, and an additional fee of $4.00 for two or more shows on the same night." But since the Club would, under the terms of the contract, continue to "purchase equipment to repair the engine, dynamo, etc.," the rent seems small indeed. Nevertheless, the directors were pleased with the arrangement. In all, forty shows were given and by the end of the summer the season had proved so successful both as to good management and well selected films that the McCleans were asked to continue on through September and possibly longer.

Encouraged by the prospect of further remuneration from

the picture shows and the promise of a "substantial sum" from the Market Fair of 1921, the directors considered the finances of the Club to be "in an excellent state." Furthermore, Miss Eames, chairman of the Motion Picture Committee, was authorized to sign a new contract with the Mc-Cleans for the coming season, beginning in June 1923. Then without a word of explanation an entry in the November minutes of 1922 reads: "The entire Equipment for Motion Pictures as installed in Firemen's Hall was sold to the Woodstock Fire Company for the sum of $700.00."

Another change in the Club's affairs was recorded without comment after it had taken place: "The library room has been moved from quarters on the State Road to a studio in the rear of same. New shelves have been added & books reclassified. The moving was greatly facilitated by the kindness of Mr. Neher."

The studio, a new white frame building owned by George Neher, was an attractive place with plenty of room for tables, chairs, the librarian's desk, and the 3000 books that had been sorted according to general subject matter: "fiction and books of more solid character."

With the library nicely settled in new and better quarters, the time seemed ripe for another try at persuading the town to contribute at least a little something toward running expenses. At the October meeting in 1923 a committee was appointed to "approach the town in behalf of the library." Doubtless the two committeemen, Mr. Neher and Mr. Herrick, did their best but the stern-faced members of the Town Board based their refusal on what must have appeared to them a watertight excuse. They replied that "The Town Board has no authority to appropriate money without the vote of the tax payer."

When the disappointed committee reported the failure of its mission at the next meeting, which was not held until June, 1924, the directors' reaction was the appointment of still another committee (Francis Clough, Mrs. Clara Park, and Mr. J. L. Banks) "to take steps in regard to having the taxpayers vote for an appropriation for the library." Evidently the three found the assignment too difficult because four months later, in October, we find this brief entry: "No report from Committee chosen to take steps toward having a town appropriation for the Library." And there the matter rested for close to a year.

Then in June, 1925, Miss Eames and Mr. Whitehead were appointed "a committee to go before the Town Board on July 6, '25 and present the following petition:"

Whereas the need of meeting the public demands for a library in the town of Woodstock has for the past twelve years been supplied by the Directors of the Woodstock Club through their own efforts and

Whereas this library now has considerably over 3000 volumes & the approximate yearly circulation of same throughout the township is about 10,000 volumes, in view of this growth and increasing need of financial support.

We, the Directors of the Woodstock Club, do hereby petition your honorable board to provide a yearly grant of $400.00 to help pay the yearly expenses of the maintenance and development of this library.

It was a noble but fruitless effort. The Town Board blandly said it had no authority "to take action in regard to levying a tax for maintaining a library."

The Club still had a trump card to play — or so it seemed. At the meeting in June of 1925 Mr. Neher had been appointed to take immediate steps to have the Woodstock Club incorporated, and he was ready, incorporation papers in hand, at the next meeting, which was held in August. Under the watchful eye of Leslie Elwyn, notary, three copies of the document were duly signed by the directors and Mr. Elwyn was tendered a standing vote of thanks for his kindness in giving his services.

Then comes an entry that indicated, like a straw in the

wind, the direction in which the Club was heading: "Resolved that a committee be appointed to investigate a place for housing the library, i.e., Mr. Victor Lasher's house for one. Carried. The chair appointed Miss Eames and Mr. Whitehead." This was followed by another resolution authorizing the Secretary "to write to the State Librarian in Albany for information regarding what assistance is given by the State to small libraries."

9

The Lasher Property

Mr. Lasher, the town's highly regarded undertaker, lived a short distance from the Club's first headquarters on the State Road, and the house in question was next door to his.

This white frame building was not large but it did have a good-size room with two windows overlooking the big open field in front. The two rooms along the west side of the house had served as the waiting room and office of Dr. Larry Gilbert Hall, the original owner of the house. Many years later they were converted by the Lashers into an apartment rented at times to summer tenants willing to make do without running water and an inside toilet. Since there was a separate entrance, tenants could come and go without disturbing those in the rest of the house.

"If the library doesn't need all the space for books at first," Mr. Lasher told the committee, "the Ell could be subrented." And when asked why the apartment was called "the Ell," he explained that the two rooms formed an L-shaped structure because the room in the rear was wider than the one in front. Mr. Whitehead said he liked the Colonial-type fireplace — it would give the library a homey look. "You could tell that the house is very old," he added, "the floor boards are unusually wide."

As secretary of the Club, Miss Eames took her job seriously; her entries in longhand are legible and concise. From minutes dated August 27, 1926, we learn that when she and Mr. Whitehead had inspected Mr. Lasher's "cottage," they had found it "feasible with the necessary alterations which Mr. Lasher was willing to make" and that the rent would be

"$250 per annum and that if certain alterations were made it would be necessary to take the house for 5 years."

Believed to be one of the oldest houses in the village, it had been purchased by Victor Lasher's grandfather in 1885 following the death of Catherine Longyear Hall, the widow of Dr. Hall, who had died in 1836. Therefore the house may have been a century old at the time the Club considered renting it.

Without reaching a decision the directors turned next to Albany's reply to their request for information about State aid to small libraries. A booklet entitled *Libraries, Public and Association* had been enclosed and after studying it carefully they voted to authorize the secretary to take steps to have the Club registered under the Regents. And again they appointed a committee, this time Miss Alice Wardwell, the president, and Mr. Whitehead, the treasurer, to go before the Town Board at the regular meeting in September (1925) to request money for the library, in accordance with handbook 8, part C: "An association library may receive aid from local taxation when registered by the Regents." That was the key phrase.

The directors may have been convinced that they were at long last on the right track. But just to be on the safe side the secretary was instructed to write to the Secretary of State to ask if the Woodstock Club *as at present incorporated can be incorporated by the Regents of the State of New York*" as an association library.

Not until nine months later at the next meeting, which was held in July of 1926, was the answer to the inquiry concerning incorporation read aloud and the directors learned that their present incorporation and incorporation under the Regents were "two different kinds of incorporation." In other words, the Club's present incorporation applied to business matters only. A library could become a member of the State system of libraries only when a charter or its temporary equivalent was granted by the Board of Regents.

"Resolved that action in regard to incorporating under State Regents," the secretary wrote, "be laid on table."

Having found that door locked, so to speak, the Club decided to concentrate on getting the town to contribute a few hundred dollars every year. But rather than make another direct appeal and risk another blunt refusal, the directors figured out a new approach. State Senator Waldon would be asked to draw up a petition to be presented to the Town Board requesting that the people of Woodstock be permitted to vote on granting an annual appropriation of $300 for the support of the library.

Senator Waldon proved to be gratifyingly prompt in complying with the Club's request, and a special meeting of the directors was called to sign the formal document prepared by the Senator's office. A careful study of the petition, however, caused one alert director to declare that, as worded, it could not be used. "Look," he said, "it calls for the support of a 'public library' and since our library is not even an association library we have no authority to present such a petition."

Everyone agreed and once again the entry in the minutes was short and to the point: "Resolved to lay on table the matter of petitioning the Town Board for financial aid."

At the Annual Meeting in October the Building Committee reported that a property referred to at the last meeting was not available, consequently "Mr. Lasher's property was recommended."

Mr. Lasher, who was among those present, had been waiting more than a year for the Club to make up its mind, and now that a decision had been reached he said he would put "the exterior of the building in perfect repair, paint same, install electricity and make the adjustment in the building making it suitable for library purposes." As for the rent, he added, "it would not be in excess of $300.00 a year on a 5-year lease."

After a lengthy discussion the members voted to accept Mr. Lasher's terms. And with this the Club took a notable step toward its goal: the founding of the Woodstock Library.

10

Every Penny Will Be Welcome

The lease was signed on November 30, 1926, and clause 6 stated that "the tenant has the option of purchasing all of said property at the expiration of five years from the date hereof, for the sum of five thousand dollars. . . ."

Well before the work of remodelling the building and installing the many book shelves had been completed, the president, Alice Wardwell, a warm, alert person who devoted countless hours to library affairs, had appointed a committee "whose duty shall be to move the library, establish it in its new quarters, make library rules and regulations and engage a librarian." *

A tall order indeed but Mrs. Lindin and the members of her committee (whoever they were) proved equal to the assignment. So did the Publicity Committee. The letter it wrote and distributed was both informative and interesting. "Every penny will be welcome," it says persuasively. Here it is in full:

Friends:

The Woodstock Library needs your support. We possess a collection of books of which any community might be proud. But for several years now, through lack of funds, these books have been housed in cramped and uncomfortable quarters where many of us did not even know where to find them. The Committee in charge of the Library has decided that it is time that Woodstock had a suitable library and it believes that through everyone's support and co-operation such a Library can be obtained and maintained. Consequently they have taken a five year

---

* Bruce Herrick, librarian for the past six years, had resigned.

lease on the charming old Hall House on the State Road opposite the former League Studio. This seems an ideal location for a Library, being accessible, and just far enough from the highway to be assured quiet. The interior has been altered to suit the needs of a Library. Most of the partitions on the ground floor have been removed, making a spacious, airy interior with plenty of room for book-racks, chairs and tables. The house has been wired and a Heatrola [the trade name for a currently popular type of kerosene stove] installed.

It is the desire of the Committee to make this a hospitable gathering place for the entire community, old and young. We especially wish to attract the young people and encourage the habit of reading and the familiarity with books, and with this idea in mind, one corner is to be devoted exclusively to the children, their books and interests. Heretofore there has been no co-operation between the school and the Library. Mr. Eighmey, who is now a member of the committee, will encourage his pupils to avail themselves of the Library in every way. A committee consisting of Miss Moncure and Mrs. Mattson, will have this section as their special care and will devote one afternoon a week to the children and will try and have a constructive program including story telling and reading aloud stories, poetry, etc.

All of this has entailed a very considerable outlay of money, but the Committee believes that Woodstock is ready and willing to support a Library worthy of its collection of books, and in keeping with its growth and development in other directions. But it is essential that EVERYONE should do his share in making this a permanent possession. The budget, which is most conservative, is as follows:

Rent	$300.00
Fuel	65.00
Electricity	12.00
Cleaning	50.00
Books	100.00
Periodicals	50.00
Salary of Librarian	300.00
	$877.00

41

It is the desire of the Committee to increase the salary of the librarian at least for the summer months, and we feel that we must count upon at least $1,000.00 per year to meet expenses. This means that we have each got to reach in our pockets and make a contribution. Every penny will be welcome. We would rather have a small amount from every home in the village than a few large contributions from a limited number. We want this to be a Public Library in the real sense of the word, owned and maintained "by the people and for the people."

Will you not subscribe for as much as you feel that you can possibly afford? You will find enclosed a pledge card which we hope you will fill out and return as soon as possible to the treasurer, Mr. R. R. Whitehead, Woodstock, N.Y. for we want to know how much of an increase of salary we can promise our librarian. The payment of any pledge of one dollar or over constitutes you a member of the Woodstock Club and entitles you to the Library privileges.

Non-members taking books must pay $1.00 as security which will be refunded when through taking books, and they must pay 5 cents per week per book. Members who have paid $1.00 receive a card and may take books free.

How could anyone resist such an appeal and for so worthy a cause! The drive may have been highly successful, but there is no way of knowing, for there is not a word about it in the minutes. The following September, however, the treasurer's report listed two savings accounts totaling more than $800 in addition to the checking account. So, by one means or another, the Club was making ends meet.

PART TWO : 1927-1951

11

The New Librarian; A Memorial Plaque

On the afternoon of Friday, March 4, 1927, a clear, sharply cold day, a reception was held to celebrate the opening of the Woodstock Club's library in its new quarters. About fifty people attended and refreshments were served by the ladies of the Women's Club of Woodstock. Probably more than a few of the guests noticed the lingering smell of fresh paint but were too polite to mention it. Undoubtedly, however, there was some guarded, quiet talk about the reason the opening had been postponed a day: "With his funeral going next door it wouldn't do, you know. Not when it was one of the trustees who had died, Westley France."

Very much in evidence that day was the new librarian, Edith Macomb, a retired art teacher who, for several years, had been spending her summers in a converted barn-studio near Rock City Corners. While she had been living in France her painting had been highly conventional in style; but after coming to Woodstock and studying under the modern painter, Andrew Dasburg (who had exhibited in the famous Armory show of 1913), her work had undergone a drastic change, though her friends insisted that it had lost none of its charm.

The Club could not afford a trained librarian and Miss Macomb was willing to try her hand at it because it was, she had been told, a part-time job: only three afternoons a week from three to six.

In order to provide a place for the children that they could call their own, the northeast corner of the room had been partly partitioned off with bookcases, and the House

45

Committee had been empowered to have a low table and benches made for the "children's room," as it was called, a nook that would prove very popular with the young fry. Under the revised bylaws, junior members "consisting of persons under sixteen years of age" would pay yearly dues of 50 cents, but would have no power to vote.

After a vote of thanks was extended to Mrs. Lindin and her assistants for so ably moving and re-establishing the library in its new quarters, eight new trustees * for the "next two ensuing years were nominated and duly elected." One name in this particular group would be long remembered — that of Mrs. Alice Thompson, the new chairman of the Library Committee.

All went smoothly for the next few weeks. While seated at a desk between the two front windows, Miss Macomb could check out books — as many as twenty-seven in a single day — collect overdue fines, and keep an eye on the room as a whole. At the meeting in June, the secretary was authorized to write to Bruce Herrick asking him to reconsider his resignation as a trustee "in view of his past interest & service in behalf of the library." This was followed by a motion "to sell the 1881 Edition of the *Encyclopaedia Britannica* to the best possible advantage."

Then out of the blue, it seems, the trustees voted that the library hours be changed, that it should be open daily "from 4 to 8 p.m., giving the librarian an extra hour from 3 to 4 for cataloging, etc." Not a word about an assistant. Yet how could even the most willing librarian be expected to forego dinner day after day until she had locked up and left at eight in the evening? Miss Macomb, who was present, did not protest. She tended to be a little overweight and the prospect of a late meal after the long walk home may have seemed unimportant. Be that as it may, a second look at the resolution was taken at the meeting in July and the fol-

* No longer called directors.

lowing schedule was adopted: "Librarian's hours and salary: June 15th to Sept. 15th, 3–7 daily except Sunday & Monday @ $60.00 per month; Sept. 15th to June 15, 3 hrs. on Friday and Saturday each @ $20.00 a month." The final entry in the minutes that day reads: "Report from the President in regard to a Bazaar and rummage sale to be held at the library on Thurs. July 28th."

There is no record of how much was made that Thursday in July but the Club seemed to be doing well financially. At the September meeting the treasurer reported the following balances: "Kingston Trust Co. Interest account $324.82; Saugerties Interest account $539.70; Kingston Trust Co. checking acct. $291.95; total $1156.47." But by far the best of all was the check for $5000.00 received from Mrs. Weyl — the exact amount for the purchase from Victor Lasher of the building and land, a plot 100 feet wide and 150 feet deep.

All correspondence between the board and Mrs. Weyl that led to this move on her part is missing, but the letters we do have speak for themselves. The library building would be a memorial to the late Walter Weyl.

In her letter of "profound gratitude," dated September 27, 1927, the Secretary wrote:

My dear Mrs. Weyl:

At the meeting of the Trustees held last evening, your check for five thousand dollars was formally turned over to the Woodstock Club, Inc. for the purpose of purchasing the building now occupied by the Library.

It is futile to try to express in words what this means to the Club and to the entire town. On all sides we hear "It is the finest thing that has ever happened to Woodstock!"

We shall endeavor to live up to your expectation of us in growing wisely and well.

Mr. Banks will make us a bronze plate about ten by twelve inches, for the exterior of the building; and will you write out for us what you would like to have put on it?

In expressing the profound gratitude of the Trustees of the club for your most generous gift, I am sure that it is an expression in which the whole community joins us.

Sincerely,

Marion G. Eames, *Secy.*
Woodstock Club, Inc.

Eager to express their appreciation in every possible way, the board also voted to make Mrs. Weyl a life member of the library and an honorary trustee. And enclosed with the letter notifying Mrs. Weyl of this was a drawing by Mr. Banks that showed how the wording, chosen by Mrs. Weyl, would appear on the plaque. In her reply, dated November 16, 1927, she wrote:

My dear Miss Eames:
That was indeed a sweet thing of the Trustees of the Woodstock Club — I am indeed happy to be an Honorary Trustee. The drawing is just right. I have no criticisms and am returning the drawing immediately.

Sincerely,

Bertha Poole Weyl

The plaque, now in the vestibule of the Library, is a source of pride for all those who know its history. It reads:

IN MEMORY
OF WALTER WEYL
ONE OF THE FOUNDERS OF THIS LIBRARY
WHO LOVED WOODSTOCK
AND ITS PEOPLE
1927

Mrs. Weyl was first of many honorary trustees — we shall come to another quite soon — and because the Woodstock Club, Inc. was not subject to rules under which a *chartered* library functions, Mrs. Weyl's status as a trustee remained unchanged: she would continue to cast a vote at the meetings.

12

The Winter Replacement, Alice Thompson

At the time Miss Macomb accepted the post of librarian, she told Mrs. Lindin that it was her established custom to leave Woodstock by December first; therefore a replacement for the winter months would have to be found. Luckily Mrs. Lindin had no difficulty at all in locating a substitute: the chairman of the Library Committee, Alice Thompson, readily agreed to take over while Miss Macomb was away. And unlike Edith Macomb, Mrs. Thompson had some previous experience in the field, having worked for a while in a library in Miami, Florida, probably as a volunteer.

In appearance the two were as opposite as the poles: Edith Macomb was a large deliberate woman; Alice Thompson was small and energetic.

In April of 1928 Miss Macomb returned to Woodstock prepared to resume her duties as librarian, one being the writing of the report she would read aloud at the next trustees' meeting. The paper, still clipped in with the minutes is headed "May 21, 1928, Woodstock Club, Inc.," and reads:

At the Annual Meeting of a year ago we reported approximately 4085 books on our shelves. Since May of last year we have added 518 books as follows: By purchase and rebinding old stock, 265; by gifts, 253; therefore the total number of books at the present date is 4603. Circulation from May 21, 1927 to May 21, 1928: Books 1721, Magazines 1000, total 2731. There are approximately 175 active readers of which 37 are juniors.

Miss Macomb, it should be noted, did not use the name Woodstock Library. Officially it was still the Woodstock Club, Inc.

Now that the building belonged to the Club, the board devoted much thought to what should be done about the apartment known as the Ell. Most of the trustees felt that if the place were rented the money could be put to good use. One applicant, however, who had offered to sign a lease for a year was refused because she was unwilling to pay more than $12 a month. The need for quiet during library hours was another consideration.

After a motion was made and carried the secretary wrote: "Resolved: to prohibit renting or sub-renting of Ell to families with children under 16 yrs. of age & that all tenants must keep quiet during library hours."

Before the meeting adjourned the members voted to make Mr. Whitehead an honorary trustee, and in his letter of acceptance he expressed his appreciation and thanks. Like Mrs. Weyl, he was happy to be thus honored.

That summer the Entertainment Committee announced two benefits to be given for the Library: a concert by the Woodstock String Quartet at the League Studio Hall on August 11; and on August 27 a moving picture at Firemen's Hall entitled "The Tempest." It featured John Barrymore.

"The library will receive half the proceeds of each performance," the chairman, Mrs. Lindin, said. "Another project that I hope will be successful," she told the trustees, "is our special rummage table at the Market Fair each Saturday morning during August."

All too often we do not know how successful such benefits were, but this time we do, thanks to the treasurer's report. Harvey Todd wrote: "Sales and entertainments, $269.20."

Ever on the lookout for ways in which to extend the activities and usefulness of the library, Miss Macomb proposed holding a party in September for the children "to celebrate Book Week." The idea appealed to Mrs. Thompson. She helped spread the word that prizes would be given for the best poster and the best essay about books. "The response was most gratifying," Miss Macomb said in her report.

"About fifty children came and many posters were submitted. Twelve excellent papers were read aloud and the children themselves judged the winner — an essay called 'Why I like Books.' Ice cream and cake were graciously donated by Miss Wardwell."

The party ended on a high note with a play staged by Mrs. Thompson's two daughters, Betty and Noël.

In December the board decided that rather than pay Mrs. Thompson $20 a month during the rest of the winter she would receive three dollars a day. For the work of cataloging the books, to be done outside library hours, she would be paid an additional dollar an hour. And since she had served as an assistant to the librarian in charge of cataloging at Miami, Alice Thompson did know a little something about what is actually a highly technical job. She must have devoted much time to her new assignment. The minutes dated May 28, 1929 read: "The card catalog was begun and nearly 1000 cards were made out for the Fiction under the names of the authors, more than 100 hours were spent for which the Library has paid $50. This means that more than 1000 were listed as there are several books usual [*sic*] under one author's name."

Since the original agreement had been a dollar an hour for cataloging, we can only wonder why Mrs. Thompson received only $50 for "more than 100 hours." Even the entry on the next page leaves us puzzled: "Mrs. Thompson was given an additional sum of $25 for her valuable work on the Catalogue."

13

A Special Section for Art Books:
Three Hundred Leaflets

In the spring of 1929 when it was time to renew Edith Macomb's contract for the coming year, one of the trustees, Marion Bullard, was asked to talk things over with Miss Macomb and learn from her what she thought about the work hours and the sort of work that would best fit the needs of the library. Miss Macomb, who was enjoying her job, responded to Mrs. Bullard's questioning with enthusiasm. "First, we need the largest appropriation for books the library can afford," she began. "After all, it's the presence of books on the shelves that is the greatest factor in attracting new readers."

Mrs. Bullard jotted down, "More money for books."

"And I think it a pity to rent the Ell," Miss Macomb continued, "when the space could be used to such advantage for a quiet reading room and a special section for art books and prints — portfolios containing prints of the work by our distinguished artists and illustrators. . . ."

"Some of the trustees think the art books could be kept in the small room on the southeast corner," Mrs. Bullard reminded her.

"But that's actually an entry hall," Miss Macomb protested. "I don't see why the front door is kept locked and everyone has to come in the side door. I also think we should have a special Woodstock shelf for volumes of poetry and prose by our writers, and a shelf for books about the history of this village," she added.

"Are there any particular books you think the library should buy?" Mrs. Bullard asked.

"Yes, we should get sets of Ibsen and Bernard Shaw, as well as a life of Beethoven and Roger Fry's *Transformation* and a life of Cezanne. Also *Cahiers d'Arts* but that would have to be ordered direct from Paris."

When the salary was discussed Miss Macomb modestly said that "seventy-five cents an hour for a four-hour day would be satisfactory."

The trustees were pleased with Mrs. Bullard's "very full, comprehensive report and instructed the secretary to file it." And much to Miss Macomb's satisfaction, all of the books she proposed were purchased, but what she had said about not renting the Ell was filed without comment.

During the summer the Entertainment Committee arranged for a series of talks for the benefit of the library. "Library Teas and Talks," Mrs. Lindin called them in her report. "There seemed so many interesting people living among us," she said, "whose various talents were scarcely suspected by many of us. On being approached, these tired and busy people, many of them on their summer vacations, unhesitatingly responded with utmost generosity. The talks were held in various private homes which in their turn were offered in the same spirit of helpfulness and cooperation. The different speakers were: Professor James T. Shotwell, Georges Barrere [of the Maverick, a well known flutist], Orville H. Peets, Konrad Cramer, John Kingsbury and Dr. Joshua Rosett and the people at whose houses the talks were held were: Mrs. [Elizabeth] Gjodvad, Mrs. Harrison, Mrs. Neilson T. Parker, Mrs. Cecil Chichester, Mrs. Lindin, and the Viletta. All were well attended, and the receipts [$395] were higher than the committee hoped for."

It was not until the June meeting of 1930 that the members learned how busy Miss Macomb and her winter replacement, Mrs. Thompson, had been during the past year. "Circulation has increased by 1106," Miss Macomb reported, "to reach a new high of 5851. In March alone — although the library was open only two days a week — 664 books

were given out. That's almost *double* the number in March
of the previous year. There's been a *slight* increase in membership, 290 this year, 240 last year, with 40 children taking
out books." Under the heading "New Business" there were
two items of special interest. Now that Mrs. Thompson had
become the winter librarian, she felt she should offer her
resignation as a trustee of the Club. This was accepted but
with regret. Miss Wardwell then reported a "generous gift of
$200" received from the president of the Market Fair, Clara
Chichester, adding that "since contributions from the Market
Fair are given to several Woodstock institutions, the turn of
the Library may not come again for two or three years."

Before turning the gavel over to the newly elected president, Mrs. Gjodvad, Miss Wardwell addressed the meeting
and the secretary *pro tem,* Alice Strain, hastily took notes.

"She spoke of the important work laid on the Trustees,
saying that the Library is a very unusual one and the duties
of its management are complicated as it is constantly growing in importance. She thought a folder should be sent out
with a view to increasing membership. She added that both
Miss Macomb and Mrs. Thompson had given much time &
thought to the work of the library in addition to their regular hours of paid work — that Miss Moncure's hours of reading to the children are invaluable, leading them on to what
is finest in literature. . . .'

The folder proposed by the president was printed and 300
were distributed throughout the village. On the front is a
hand-attached reproduction of a delightful pencil sketch by
Orville Peets which shows the old building and the towering
leafless trees of wintertime. What the leaflet has to say about
the history of the library from its beginning is somewhat surprising, however: The Club, it states, conducted and fi-
nanced "not only a library but several other activities for the
benefit of the people of Woodstock and the vicinity. An
athletic association and an organization of visiting nurses
. . . were included in the framework of the Club. . . ."

Since the Club's minutes covering all aspects of its activities speak only of hiring a nurse "in cases of necessity," that seems a far cry from "an organization of visiting nurses," and not once is there any reference to an athletic association or even plans for one. When Mrs. Martin Comeau (the former Marion Eames) was interviewed in 1969, she stated categorically that the Club had never sponsored an athletic association. If she had been present when the leaflet was being written, it would have been more accurate.

Another example of how misinformation gets a toehold in the history of an organization is what the leaflet has to say next: "The sum received from the sale of the motion-picture machine was never formally allotted to the Library." Of course the $700 received by the Club from the Woodstock Fire Company for its entire motion-picture outfit was not formally allotted to the library because the Club and its library were by now actually one and the same.

"Although our legal name of the Library remains the same," the leaflet continues, "it had been found preferable to omit, where possible, all reference to the Woodstock Club." Then comes the explanation: "To make this change of name would involve some expense, and though it may be done later other needs are more pressing."

Fortunately the Club had a comfortable backlog of cash on hand — in all, $1801.38. It's library was not only paying its way but after adding up outlay and income it would still be $67.50 ahead of the game.

Here is the treasurer's report for 1929 as it appeared on the back of the booklet:

Received During the Year:

Subscriptions [membership dues]	$624.00
Teas	395.00
Market Fair	200.00
Rent [the Ell]	110.00
Sale — Winter Book Fund	84.34
Incidentals	7.00
Charges [overdue fines]	27.24
Total Receipts	1467.58

Paid Out:

Salaries	$494.00
Cataloguing Books	170.75
Binding Books	8.60
Books and Magazines	511.27
Card Cabinet	27.65
Shelves	28.45
Other Supplies	55.04
Electric Lights	11.00
Insurance	15.13
Taxes [real estate]	55.91
Miscellaneous	22.60
Total Expenses	1400.49

"The $624.00 for subscriptions is a credible amount," the leaflet goes on, "and several contributions might be included under this head; but it will be necessary to double this sum before the Library will be free from the need of counting upon exceptional — and unfortunately uncertain — means of raising money."

"Uncertain means of raising money." Those words written more than forty years ago, before the Town Board had contributed anything whatever, and before the *first* of the long series of library fairs, have echoed down through the years to be heard again and again when other trustees were trying to figure out new ways of raising money for the library.

14

"Friends of the Woodstock Library"

In the summer of 1930 someone did hit upon a fresh approach. The library mailed folders which stressed the importance of Woodstock as an art center and the library's "need of a specially fine section of books on music and the plastic arts." But since such books would be too expensive to be purchased from the general book fund, the folder said, those who may wish to become "Friends of the Woodstock Library" by presenting such books, prints, or scores, or contributing large or small amounts to a "special fund for the Art Section" would have their names and contributions "recorded in a book available for inspection at any time."

On the back of the folder were a few titles which might, it was suggested, serve as a guide: Coomaraswamy, *Rajput Painting 16th to 19th century* $100; Pisanello, *Drawings* (1927) $17.50; George Bellows, *Paintings* $17.50; Gauguin, *Facsimile of Sketchbook* in color $75."

It was an ambitious attempt, but from the rather wistful few lines penned by the secretary in the October minutes, the response may have been rather disappointing: "Some books have been given — some money received — it is hoped another year will show much headway." And that's the last we ever heard of it. But the two White Elephant sales, one at the Country Club, the other at the Market Fair on a Saturday morning, did very well — they brought the library $316.90.

The next entry made at the same meeting is surprising to say the least: "The division of funds by the Book Committee is of particular interest — it is noted here as it will be of help in the future — $600.00 to be expended thus:

    1 Fiction $200
    2 Juvenile $66.66
    3 Biography & Travel $66.66
    4 Philosophy, Psychology & Religion $66.66
    5 Painting, Sculpture, Crafts, Architecture $50
    6 Poetry, Music, Drama, Belles-lettres $50
    7 Science, History, Euthenics $50
    8 Magazines $50"

That is indeed a puzzler. How could a presumably informed Committee allocate money on such a basis with the cost of each catagory figured down to the last cent and with Juveniles rating more than expensive books on Art?

Before the October meeting in 1930 Miss Macomb handed the secretary a formal letter of resignation as librarian. "My very uncertain health makes this necessary. During my absence . . . Mrs. Thompson has ably carried on the work and I heartily recommend her as my successor."

Mrs. Thompson's equally formal application "for the position of your librarian" was also read aloud by the secretary and the trustees made their vote of acceptance unanimous. The new librarian was familiar with all aspects of the work. Moreover, she was gentle-voiced, self-effacing, and well liked.

Once again, the following spring, the board found itself debating the question: what should be done about the Ell? In the fall it had been rented to a "temporary" tenant for $15 a month and had then stood empty for most of the winter. Evidently no one said, "What a pity to have the place vacant when the library so needs extra space." Instead, one of the trustees hit upon a practical solution: "I'm sure," she said, "a furnished apartment could be rented easily." The idea met with instant approval and before the meeting broke up there had been offers from almost everyone present to donate "all that would be needed in the way of furnishings."

After being thoroughly cleaned and freshly painted, the "nicely furnished Ell" was rented in the summer of 1931 to two quiet ladies. For their two-months' stay they paid $70, netting the library the handsome profit of $41.44. "We loved it," the younger of the two told us years later. "I used to sit on the front steps of the Ell and watch the traffic go by on the State Road, but during library hours we tiptoed round and talked in whispers."

15

The First Library Fair

If this short entry in the September minutes of 1931 were all we have to go on little would be known about the first of the library's annual Fairs: "Mrs. Weyl, Chairman of the Entertainment Committee, spoke of the very successful 'Country Fair' in August which realized the sum of $534.31 and suggested that a sale of this kind be made an annual event." But thanks to the energetic Marion Bullard, in charge of publicity, we are not left in the dark.

The first write-up, a half-column story, printed on page 1 of *The Woodstock Press,* Friday, July 31, 1931, was headed "Country Fair in August, For Benefit of Woodstock Library On Library Grounds — Those in Charge of Booths."

A meeting of those actively concerned in the annual summer benefit for the Woodstock Library was held last week at the residence of Mrs. Walter Weyl, chairman, and the first plans laid. It was decided to name it "The Country Fair" and to make the occasion much more than a rummage sale (White Elephant) originally talked of.

The Country Fair will take place on the Library grounds, Wednesday, August 26th, to avoid any interference with the regular Saturday morning Market Fair.

Further plans will be announced in the *Press* as soon as they are completed. Many amusing and entertaining features will be added to the customary tables and booths and these, with requests from the various chairmen as to what is wanted for their tables, will be told next week, or as soon as available.

In charge of booths: Table Decorations, Mrs. Neil Ives; Kitchen Utensils, Mrs. Carl Eric Lindin; Books, Mrs. John Carlson and

Mrs. Miska Petersham; Hat and Gown Shop, Mrs. Henry Matt-
son; Dime Booth, Miss Joan Stagg and Miss Karen Lindin;
Flower Shop, Mrs. Martin Schutze; Delicatessen, Miss Margaret
Shotwell and Miss Helen Shotwell; Men's Shop, Mrs. Alfeo
Faggi and Mrs. Neilson T. Parker; General Utility, Mrs. Walter
Weyl.

The arrangement of the grounds is in charge of Miss Anita
Smith, and the publicity and posters, Mrs. Marion Bullard and
Mr. Albert Heckman.

The next write-up, dated Friday, August 14, was also a
feature story in the *Press*. Under the heading "Country Fair
Plans Develop — So, It's Heigh Ho! Come To Our Fair on
Library Lawn in August."

It begins by repeating much of what has been said about
the booths but goes into greater detail, giving the telephone
numbers of the various chairmen. For example: "Mrs. Petersham asks all who have books, especially detective novels
and children's books, they are willing to contribute, to
telephone her (Tel. Woodstock 88) and she will call for
them. . . ."

Again, the following Friday (August 21) the *Press* ran an
even longer front page account: "Country Fair Plans Perfect
— But Look Below For Items You May Contribute To Make
Library Benefit A Success."

On Tuesday afternoon, August 18, the chairmen of all booths
met on the lawn of the Library to discuss final plans and arrangements for the Country Fair to be held on Wednesday August 26.
The Country Fair will be held from two until six o'clock.

Miss Anita Smith is in charge of the grounds and has been
dyeing material in vivid colors for banners. Henry Lee McFee
has been assisting Miss Smith in color plans. Mr. Frederick [Fred
Dana] Marsh, well-known mural painter, who is spending the
summer in Woodstock, is doing a large poster for the Country
Fair to be hung on the grounds. . . . Mrs. Lindin also asked
that those who have recently acquired electric irons be kind
enough to give their old flat irons to the Fair. . . . Mrs. Walter

Weyl has gowns and hats and asks especially for contributions. Mrs. Weyl's telephone number is Woodstock 25. . . . If the weather interferes, the Country Fair will be held the next clear day.

On the same page in the next column, headed "No Market Fair" is the following:

Due to Saturday morning's heavy rainfall no Market Fair was held, and the temporary suspension marked the first Saturday morning this summer that weather has interfered with the weekly bazaar.

In the meantime a short article appeared in the *New York Times* about the Fair. It stated when and where the Country Fair would be held, and went on to name those who would supervise the tables and booths. "There will be many original booths erected," the article continued, "and a variety of goods displayed from pictures, lithographs, art books and embroideries down to pies and cakes."

A happening such as this in Woodstock, the home town of many famous artists in those days, was news in New York's leading newspaper!

The weather continued to interfere. On Friday, August 28, the day after the Fair, the account in the *Press* was not long. Headlined "Country Fair Is Rained On — And So Remainder of Saleable Articles Were Offered Thursday — Results Successful," it reported:

Spasmodic thundershowers on Wednesday afternoon all but ruined the long-planned and long-awaited Country Fair, the Woodstock Library benefit held on the Library green.

The booths were all colorful and held many articles of decorative and utilitarian value, and the rain which dampened the large attendance failed to dampen spirits in any manner.

Trading was active, even the old beggar lady and the wandering minstrels caught substantial sums in the pennies and dimes and larger amounts tossed by pitying residents into their tin cups.

Due to the breakup caused by the rain, word was quickly passed over the village that the Country Fair would be continued the following day, in order that those who contributed might see the Library realize a financial profit.

One old-timer remembers the grass-laced mud underfoot and how the banners, so valiantly dyed by Anita Smith, hung limp and streaked. Yet sales were brisk. "Such was the enthusiasm," Miss Smith said, "that people bought damaged garments and sodden food at fantastic prices to save the library."

In the minutes, Mrs. Weyl's short report on the Fair was followed by one from Miss Smith, chairman of the newly launched activity, the Extension Committee: "The members of the Extension Committee consist of Mrs. Thompson, Miss Margaret Shotwell, Miss Helen Shotwell and Anita Smith," she began. "We have been holding an extension library in the Willow schoolhouse once every two weeks all summer. The number of books taken out have run between eleven to thirty-two each time. The interest shown has made the venture very worthwhile and at the request of the grown-up readers as well as the children, we have decided to continue providing books throughout the winter.

"For this purpose the new teacher, Miss Berry, has consented to help us distribute the books on alternate Wednesdays right after school. The school trustee, Mrs. Walter Jessup, has cooperated with us and has shown her appreciation for our efforts in most gratifying ways. It was largely due to *her* efforts that so many *donations of food* from Willow were contributed to our Fair. Added to the fine work done by Mrs. Ashley Cooper on Miss Shotwell's committee we feel that the upper Valley helped in no small measure the success of our money-raising entertainment [the Fair]."

When the board finally got round to the troublesome question of what to do about the Ell, since once again it was standing empty, "There was a long discussion," the secretary wrote, "as to ways and means of enlarging the Library, giving a Reference Room — or quiet room for study.

"Mrs. Bullard suggested using the front room of the Ell — building on another room so that we should still have three [?] rooms to rent — others felt we should not have a tenant, but should use the Ell for Library purposes — Miss Smith suggested opening the ceiling & having a balcony on the second floor, thus using much space at present wasted." Finally Mrs. Schoonmaker moved that "a Committee be appointed to get estimates & report at a special meeting of Trustees on a later date. . . . Carried and the President appointed Mrs. Bullard, Mrs. Weyl, Mr. Neher and Mr. Frederick Marsh. . . ."

Then, at the president's request, Mrs. Thompson left the meeting so that the matter of a gift or bonus for her might be discussed. Mrs. Weyl moved that "the Librarian be given $75 from Library Funds as a mark of appreciation from the trustees for her devoted work and interest. This was unanimously carried. Adjournment followed," Mrs. Strain wrote with a flourish. It had been a very long meeting and her minutes took up more than six, closely-written pages in the bound book.

16

The Library's Certificate of Membership

Mailing out annual letters to the members, reminding them that it was time to send dues for the coming year, had long been the custom. In the spring of 1932 the following printed, one-page letter was sent to 275 members:

May 28, 1932

Dear Member:—
The Library too has felt the depression.
But we must carry on.
The renewals are due June 1st.
Will you lift your membership to as high a
denomination as you feel you can.
Sincerely,
Nancy Schoonmaker
Chairman, Membership Committee

"There is no report from the special Committee appointed to consider alterations to the Library Building," the secretary wrote during the trustees' meeting held on June 2, 1932. And that was the last entry on the subject ever recorded. Mrs. Bullard, who had been a member of that committee, made no reference to it when she gave her report as chairman of the House Committee. "The Ell is now rented to Miss Mary Wilson for fifteen dollars a month," she said, "and we had to purchase a stove for it." Quite a comedown from the $35 a month paid by the summer tenants.

Mr. Todd had been the first to point out that the library was being required by the town to pay real estate taxes. "We are an educational institution," he said, "and therefore should be *tax exempt*."

Understandably all the trustees felt that the town should contribute at least *something* toward the upkeep of the library and Mr. Bruno Zimm, the sculptor, had been asked to talk to the Board of Tax Assessors. "This board seems willing to exempt us," he reported, "*if* our renting of the Ell doesn't prevent it."

"Mr. Zimm then brought forward the matter of changing the name of the Library from Woodstock Club, Inc. to Woodstock Library," the entry continues, "and re-incorporating as a Free Association Library under New York State laws. This was fully discussed & finally Mrs. Schoonmaker moved that the Trustees recommend such changes in order to secure Tax Exemption, some financial support from the State, and other advantages. Mr. deWitt Shultis seconded this motion and suggested that a Committee be appointed to present By-Laws at the annual meeting. Mr. Zimm was appointed and the Secretary was instructed to send notice of these recommended changes to each member of the Woodstock Club to be voted upon at the annual meeting which was fixed for June 16th. The meeting then adjourned. Alice J. Strain, Sec."

A week before the meeting postcards bearing the following printed notice were in the mail:

WOODSTOCK LIBRARY

The regular annual meeting of the Woodstock Club, Inc. will be held on Thursday, June 16th at 8 p.m. in the Library. Reports will be read, trustees elected, and the following recommendations voted upon: To change the name from "The Woodstock Club, Inc." to "The Woodstock Library," and to become an Association Library under the State Laws in order to secure tax exemption and certain other advantages.

THE BOARD OF TRUSTEES
Alice J. Strain, Sec.

Note: Library hours from June 15th to Sept. 15th are 3–6 daily except Sundays, Mondays and holidays.

This history-making meeting, with Mrs. Lindin in the chair, opened sedately enough. "There were 32 members present and the usual roll call was omitted."

After the treasurer's report of receipts and expenditures for the year plus what the Club had on hand, the total was, on the whole, quite satisfactory since it was close to $1000. "In addition to the above," the secretary wrote, "Mrs. Bullard reported the sum of $41.37 received for the 'Pet Show' held in the fall — all of this except $12.00 has been spent for books on animals, their care, etc. principally for children."

What Mr. Zimm would have to say about the advantages of becoming an association library would, of course, be the high point of the meeting, but first the various committee-men were heard from: Mrs. Schoonmaker on membership: "We are making an earnest effort to increase both member-ships and dues. . . ."; then Mrs. Thompson: "There has been a marked increase in circulation. . . . The shelf for Wood-stock authors and illustrators has had several fine additions through the year. . . ."; and Miss Smith: "Good work is being done by the Extension Committee. Five schools in addition to Woodstock are being given books every two weeks. . . ."

Finally, Mr. Zimm rose to speak and there was a stir of anticipation. He began by recalling the many times in the past that the Club had discussed the subject. "In 1925," he said, "when the Club's incorporation papers were filed we thought we were eligible for incorporation by the Regents of the State of New York as an association library, but in 1926 when a reply to our application was read and we learned we were mistaken, the motion to incorporate under the Regents was laid on the table. I now move that we take from the table the resolution passed in 1925."

"This motion was carried," the minutes state. "A lively discussion followed — Mrs. Schoonmaker read a letter from Miss Hathaway [in Albany] on the subject — Miss Smith told of the success of the Free Association Library at Haines Falls."

Mr. Zimm gave very full answers to the various questions asked and finally presented the following:

WHEREAS the activities of the Library of the Woodstock Club (Incorporated since 1925) have been, in practice, the activities of a Free Association Library, without deriving any of the usual privileges or State aid legally due to such an Association Library:

And WHEREAS the circulation of books has doubled since 1929, and our loan service to the District Schools has been extended, and a further expansion of our Library facilities to better meet the growing demands upon them is greatly needed:

And WHEREAS such an Association under the Education Law is entitled to tax exemption and State Aid, provided it registers with the State University as a Free Association Library:

And WHEREAS such State aid would be extremely helpful in fulfilling our proper functions as a Library:

Therefore, Be is resolved that we hereby announce, publish and declare that at a regular legal meeting of the Woodstock Club, Inc. held this day, June 16, 1932, we have organized, conforming to the rules and regulations of the State Regents, a Free Association Library, to be known as the Woodstock Library, and that the Secretary be hereby authorized to apply to the Regents of the University of the State of New York for registration as such; and that a copy of these resolutions be forwarded to Daniel R. Spratt, Deputy Tax Commissioner at Albany.

"When this was put to vote," the entry in the minutes continues, "there were 25 ayes — 4 noes — 3 people present did not vote — so it was carried."

Why did those four object to the Club's Library changing its status? We are not told.

There was still a chance that the Board of Regents might not grant the application for membership, but many of those present that night in June must have left the meeting greatly encouraged. The small library, founded by the Woodstock Club nineteen years earlier, now seemed to have an excellent chance of becoming a tax exempt public library and in a far better position than ever before to appeal for town aid. But as the weeks slipped by with no word from Albany, the trustees became uneasy. They decided not to issue the printed report, already planned, "until our new status shall be definitely determined." Also it seemed wise to do nothing further about the revision of the bylaws until a later meeting.

Finally, Mr. Zimm was asked if he would consult "the representative" in Albany regarding any changes that should be made by the Library.

Evidently Mr. Zimm's talk with Mr. Tolman, director of the Extension Division, led to a visit of inspection of the Woodstock Library by his assistant, Mary B. Brewster who wrote in her report to Mr. Tolman:

I think the building and room now occupied by the library offer great possibilities. The art collection is excellent, not merely books about various branches, but books of drawings, pictures, details etc. As I told Mrs. Thompson, I thought the literature collection slightly weak. She agreed with me and said she was planning to round it out, as for instance, by buying more of the standard . . . poets. I thought the reference, general reference, collection rather weak considering the excellence of the rest of the collection. Mrs. Thompson assured me that it was adequate to the present demand, and that she would build it up as rapidly as necessity required. I think that is most sensible, since in that way she will build first the field that first demands it. . . ."

Since Miss Brewster did recommend that a certificate of registration be granted, it was received by Mrs. Lindin in time for her to have it framed and hung in the library before the September meeting of the Board.

17

In the Matter of Art Books

With the certificate came a letter giving encouragement and suggestions, one being that the library should be open more than two afternoons a week during the winter months. Mrs. Thompson readily agreed but extra hours would increase the budget.

"There was some discussion about the Librarian's salary," the Secretary wrote. "The Finance Committee recommended a yearly salary of $800 — this is to cover all assistance in book work of the Library, the cataloging, handling books, accession, etc. It was finally voted to pay the Librarian, Mrs. Thompson, a salary of $750 with a bonus of $50. This to cover all expenses as above to begin Jan. 1, 1933."

"All expenses?" That seems to imply that Mrs. Thompson had better round up a volunteer to return books to the shelves or lend a hand in other ways if she didn't want to pay a helper out of her own pocket.

One reason the library's collection of fine books continued to grow was due, in large part, to two of the trustees, as an article in *The Overlook,* July 2, 1932 makes quite clear:

The Woodstock library has always enjoyed a reputation as a small library with large books. This was not a measurement of size, however, but of quality. Especially in the matter of art books the library boasts a splendid collection. It includes treatises on oriental art, on ancient art, on the panorama of painting in the western world, and covers almost all phases of the subject.

And now through the generosity of Mrs. Walter Weyl and Miss Alice Wardwell it has received notable additions.

Among the titles are the seventeen volumes of the Whitney Museum's American Artists Series, and a critical introduction to American painting by Virgil Barker. There is a large portfolio of reproductions of pre-Renaissance artists. Among other titles are the following:

Van Gogh, by Fritz Knapp; Deutsche Volkskunst: Schwaben, und Bayern; Die Kunst Ostasiens, by Otto Kummel; Ostasiatische Plastik, by Carl Glaser; Afrikanische Plastik, by Carl Einstein; Urformen der Kunst, by Emil Waldman, and Der Kunst des Realismus und Impressionismus, by Karl Blossfeldt.

Later, when a check for $50 earmarked for books was received from Albany, as was customary at that time, the librarian and the Book Committee selected the titles with care, for they knew that a list of what was being purchased would be submitted to the head of the Extension Division. Albany approved, but cautioned that "several of the books be circulated *with discretion.*" How that stirs the curiosity! [6]

Despite the clear weather the Country Fair proved less successful in 1932 and Miss Shotwell, we are told, proposed holding next year's Fair in July rather than August "because there are so many other sales and entertainments in August."

Now that the Club's library had its certificate of membership (the charter would be applied for later), it was time to decide just how much of the village should be regarded as the *free* zone of the new association library, so Mrs. Lindin proposed that a special meeting be held at her house on Thursday, October 13 to consider the matter.

Mr. Elwyn arrived with a crude map he had drawn on a

6. The books may have contained reproductions of paintings of the nude. These were regarded with uneasiness by many library officials of the time. The presence in the Woodstock Library of a fine collection of books on art was a factor in causing some people to avoid the library and to discourage their children from using it. [A.E.]

large sheet of paper, and after some discussion as to whether the village green should be regarded as the center of town the group agreed to disregard the location of the green and aim instead at determining the boundaries of "the permanent population, estimated at 600."

Beginning where the Millstream Road meets "Kingston Road" the shaky red line drawn on the map that day cuts across the Saugerties Road, taking in the Country Club and the Country Club Tavern. From there it rises in a wide arc to pass George Burt's house on the Rock City Road, then swings southward down across the Bearsville Road, around Sully's mill at the foot of Ohayo Mountain Road, to wind up where it started — forming a rather lopsided circle.

This map, now yellow with age, is attached by a rusty paperclip to page 190 in the second book of minutes. Near the top of the paper on the left-hand side is a note in ink: "Library is *free* to people living within the red line — by action of Trustees Oct. 13, 1932 — Alice Strain, Sec." Added in pencil, possibly by Mr. Elwyn, are the words: "Inside red line 'Village zone' — Estimated population 525."

It was earnestly hoped that library patrons, now officially freed from paying dues, would continue to contribute to the library — all but thirteen of them did — but the trustees were taking nothing for granted. Before the meeting adjourned, Mrs. Schoonmaker moved that "the treasurer see the Supervisor, Mr. Cashdollar, to make sure that the Library is exempt from taxation in the future." It was too soon, it seemed, to mention again how welcome a contribution from the town would be. Instead, the trustees wondered aloud about ways and means "of raising money for the library this winter," but reached no decision.

18

The Provisional Charter; Fifty Dollars from the Town

The Certificate of Membership was, at best, no more than a first step along the road toward the trustees' goal: a full charter, a public library in every sense of the word. So in the summer of 1933 a formal application was drafted and signed by the twenty trustees then serving and hopefully mailed to the State Library in Albany.

This time the Board of Regents did not keep the trustees waiting: the board was unwilling to grant an absolute charter because the financial standing of the Woodstock Library was too uncertain. A provisional charter would be granted, however, with the understanding that it would be reviewed "if within five years the corporation shall acquire sufficient property available for its use and support and be maintaining, to the satisfaction of the Regents, a library of proper standing."

Unquestionably the library could not count on an annual income. The town still refused to contribute to its upkeep, and the combined returns from the annual Fairs and the membership fees fell short of the amount needed for the budget. What it could count on, however, was the unflagging attention of a group of men and women willing to devote themselves wholeheartedly to a project of such value to the community.

The provisional charter, dated October 28, 1933, arrived in November by Railway Express. It proved to be an impressive document 20 x 16 inches in size. The names of the trustees of the library and rather lengthy terms of agreement had been filled in by the calligrapher who did the expert lettering for the State Library. And the gold seal with its embossed design was indeed impressive. Even the Town Board viewed the charter with approval and for the first time contributed "from funds on hand: a check for $50." [7]

Spurred on by their new symbol of progress, the trustees discussed the need for improvements in and about the building. "A parking place seems to be the starting point," the secretary wrote in her book of minutes. "Mr. Victor Lasher kindly gives the Library permission to use some of his adjoining land, and the front door seems to be the proper entrance."

Why had the side door, facing what is now Library Lane, been used for years rather than the front entrance? Presumably because the front door opened into a short closed-off hallway from which narrow, steep stairs led to the second floor. In the minutes this hall is referred to as "the small room on the south which could be used for art books." The minutes go on: "It was moved by Mr. Shultis, seconded by Mrs. Lindin, that the front door be used eventually as the main entrance — it was carried."

The large potbellied stove, the chief source of heat for the library, was considered inadequate by the trustees who felt that a furnace should be installed, so a committee was appointed to look into various types of heaters. But not a word was said at that meeting for the "really great need for a quiet reference room." The final entry that day stated that the President was empowered "to proceed with the necessary alterations to the interior in order to make the front door a proper entrance — carried."

---

7. The reluctance of the Town Board to contribute to the library had many causes. The Socialistic beliefs of Ralph Whitehead, the library's hospitality to writers critical of some established American ways, and the nudes in its art books all combined to make Town Board members feel reluctant to antagonize conservative voters who might very well view tax support for the library as a subsidizing of immorality and treason. Besides, the library seemed to outsiders to be doing very well indeed without public support. The struggles of the trustees to keep the library functioning and solvent were invisible to most Woodstock people. [A.E.]

Mr. Zimm, having succeeded Mrs. Lindin as president, was planning to handle the matter personally in the hope of interesting "the town authorities and influential townspeople in making improvements in and around the Library building." He seems to have presented his case well. At the board meeting in November he reported "encouraging results" from his campaign: the town merchants had donated $44 and he had received "promises of sand, dirt and the use of a truck and carpenter's labor."

The trustees did not meet again for six months and the minutes dated May 10, 1943, start on page one of the third book of records. "There were 15 present," Mrs. Strain wrote, "the President Mr. Zimm in the chair. . . . In the Librarian's absence Mrs. Schoonmaker reported that the Book Committee meets once a month: new non-fiction is passed upon by the Committee, as well as the magazines; current fiction is chosen by the Librarian."

Next came Mrs. Lindin's report as chairman of the Administration Committee. She explained that when the winter tenant in the Ell had complained about the "discomfort and inconvenience" of the place the rent had been reduced, at her request, to $10.50 a month. Yet, despite the obvious inconveniences (no running water, no indoor toilet), there had been three applicants that spring: a Mrs. Brett, Betty Thompson, and Florence Webster. What had tipped the scales in Miss Webster's favor had been her offer to sign a lease for a year and in addition to share the cost of repairs and improvements.

Miss Webster had been a trustee for the past four years and from the start had devoted a lion's share of her time to library affairs. And now, to show their appreciation, the board voted unanimously to make her a "Life Member of the Library Association and Honorary Trustee." Like the two other honorary trustees, Mrs. Weyl and Mr. Whitehead, her status as an active member of the library would remain unchanged. She would continue to serve as treasurer until the end of her term and would then become president, succeeding Mr. Zimm.

How things have changed! Today the permanent, or honorary, trustee may attend board meetings (and is urged to) but it is clearly understood that he or she shall not hold office or cast a vote. Were the rules different in the 1930's? Probably not. Educational Law 226 states that the trustees may "fix the term of office and number of trustees, which shall not exceed twenty-five, or be less than five. . . ."

In Miss Webster's day there were only twenty trustees *including* honorary members, therefore the board must have considered itself well within the letter of the law. Years later, when the number of trustees was increased to twenty-four, this automatically excluded the honorary members from active participation.

The meeting closed with a vote to continue the improvements to the library by removing a partition, throwing the hall into the present reading room, and re-arranging the stacks, tables, and desk.

The following month, at the annual meeting, Mrs. Lindin made her report with characteristic modesty but also with an air of achievement. "As you can see for yourselves," she said, "we now have more room for books, better lighting for readers and a more satisfactory position for the librarian's desk. The front door is being used and Mr. Lasher has put a fine gravel path from the road to the library steps."

In other words, when the door and inner partition of the hallway had been removed, the entryway became part of the main room and the exposed space under the steep stairs was converted into a cubbyhole closet for supplies. Mrs. Thompson's desk had been moved from where it had stood for years, between the two front windows, to the east side of the room. It was now between the small closet and the side door (locked) and from this vantage point Mrs. Thompson could keep track of what was going on in the children's nook at her right and at the same time see who entered or left by the front door.

After Mrs. Lindin had completed her report, it was the librarian's turn to speak: "We now have more than eight thousand books on our shelves and these are constantly being added to and weeded out. . . ."

Before the meeting adjourned that evening two items of special interest were recorded. The first had to do with the Fair: "It was decided to hold the Country Fair in August, as usual, and Miss Harriet Goddard kindly consented to take charge of it. Mrs. [Irving] Brown suggested a dog show as one of the attractions of the Fair, and agreed to manage it." The second covered a proposal long under discussion: "The President was empowered to act upon the motion passed at the Annual Meeting in regard to the annulment of the charter of the Woodstock Club, Inc. and its property being turned over to the Woodstock Association."

The third Country Fair, held on Thursday August 23, was well attended with "throngs of people coming from miles away." Even so, the big field under the trees was not so crowded but what everyone could circulate and greet many friends. Miss Goddard had appointed Betty Brown and Margaret Ives as managers, a team that proved so efficient that they were frequently congratulated on the way they ran the show.

There were games, music, tea on the terrace, and the Pet Show in back of the library where well-known Woodstock animals — goats, roosters, rabbits, guinea pigs, frogs, parrots, cats, and dogs — competed for ribbons and prizes, with the high point of the contest being for the fastest wagging tail. The first prize went to Billy Johnson's black puppy, which was clocked at 21 wags a minute; next came Marion Bullard's Scotty, at 17 wags a minute. And what caused roars of laughter was Bob Watt's Sealyham. He plunked himself down on his tail and rated zero. There were prizes for the most beautiful pet (a rabbit) and the pet with the most spots (a Dalmatian).

The Fair had thirty departments ranging from Toys (it took in $40) to Women's Clothing ($130), Food ($70), and a game, Ring Toss ($20). Miss Smith's display of herbs from her Stonecrop Shop did less well — only 75 cents.

At the September meeting of the board, Miss Goddard reported a total of $735 netted in one afternoon — a record. And at this same meeting Julia Leaycraft was appointed secretary by the president, in place of Mrs. Strain, resigned. Mrs. Leaycraft must have taken copious notes in pencil from which to work, but she doubtless had a retentive memory as well since her businesslike, typed reports cover each meeting in detail from start to finish. For example:

"Miss Doughty said that the State Library had replied to her letter asking if it would be possible for Albany to send a professional librarian to Woodstock to make an inventory of the books and authors' cards. She was told that Miss LeFever thought it would not take longer than a week if we could give her five or six intelligent assistants. Our card catalog really needs overhauling, Miss Doughty said, and in this way it would cost us very little — just what Miss LeFever's stay at the hotel amounts to. Then, later on, when there is an unemployed librarian on relief — on TERA [Temporary Emergency Relief Administration] — she could work on the subject cards . . . the committee feels that cataloguing the Library is of prime importance."

The next meeting was held in December and because Miss Doughty was out of town, Mrs. Schoonmaker, a member of the Book Committee, reported for her. "The plan," she said, "to have a librarian from Albany go over the card catalog was carried out in October. All the books have been sorted, special and regular markings placed on the backs which were then shellaced. The title catalog is finished as well as the greater part of the author catalog. Volunteers are meeting regularly each week to complete this work and the subject cards have been started. Thus far it has cost us only a hundred and seventeen dollars. Haines Falls spent six hundred dollars on their catalog and we have a much larger library."

Here indeed was a feather in the Woodstock Library's cap — or so it seemed at the time. Not until the following summer, however, when a professional librarian devoted five weeks to weeding out mistakes would the truth of the matter be revealed, as we shall disclose presently.

19

The Woodstock Shelf; Books for "Hungry Readers"

Snow, more snow, then sleet and ice — the winter of 1934–35 was one for staying at home as much as possible. When asked if the library was very cold at night during the sub-zero weather, Miss Webster replied that the temperature had never gone below forty-five degrees because of the fire in the coal stove. We can picture her, lighted candle in hand, going from her apartment in the Ell into the cold, silent library to inspect the thermometer.

The board meeting, scheduled for January, was postponed until May and by eight o'clock on Thursday evening, fourteen trustees had arrived, ready for President Zimm to call the meeting to order. Most of the reports dealt with routine matters. The chairman of the Administration Committee, Alice Owen, said that Roy Reynolds had agreed to stay on as janitor but he didn't think he was being paid enough, only two dollars a week for all he was expected to do: take care of the fires (coal for the stove, wood for the fireplace — an everyday job in the winter), and shovel snow. He was also supposed to sweep and dust and put away books.

Miss Doughty read from her typed notes: "I have been asked to determine what the Book Committee thinks about the Woodstock shelf. Well, there seems to be a difference of opinion about the famous shelf. A few thought it should be done away with entirely, others did not. One member suggested that any writer who visited here or who spent a summer here should be included, but the majority felt that the Woodstock shelf should represent writers whose interests were closely connected with Woodstock and, when put to a vote, the following ruling was passed: A writer whose work is represented on the Woodstock shelf must own a home in Woodstock Township, or vote in Woodstock, or have lived within the Township for five seasons, not necessarily consecutive."

What a ruling! Today a local writer or artist who donates his published books to the library's special shelf is not asked if he owns or rents the place where he is living, or if his interests are "closely connected witih Woodstock." He may well be more interested in Timbuktu. Even so his books are added to the evergrowing Woodstock Authors' and Illustrators' Shelf.

"You already know about the splendid work that was being done on the catalog last fall," she continued, "but the Book Committee thinks we should open the subject again with Albany. By this time we may be able to get a trained librarian on relief to work on our subject cards — they really can't be done by volunteers."

"Miss Doughty was authorized to contact the State Library again," Mrs. Leaycraft wrote.

Next came Anita Smith's report. She always spoke with ease and the trustees enjoyed listening to her. "The Extension Committee has enlarged its activities this year," she began. "We are not only serving the schools but are distributing books to families unable to travel to the Library. . . . Miss Webster has assumed the responsibility of taking books to adults upon request and one farmer's wife in Lake Hill told me she was so grateful. She had read a hundred books, she said, since October and didn't know how she could have survived the long winter without them. Her choice at first was for fiction but by the end of the winter she was devouring more serious non-fiction reading. One farmer has been spending his winter evenings reading economics, evolution, physics, etc., and he has asked Miss Webster about the possibilities of his taking a real course of study next winter.

"Another case of meeting a real need has been evidenced

by the gratitude expressed by one of our intellectuals who, having become isolated on a mountain in Willow, found this library service invaluable. It is the hope that this particular work of taking books to hungry readers may be continued another year."

20

More Penny Pinching; The New Catalog

In July the Executive Committee took a rather drastic step. Here is the letter it wrote and sent to the librarian:

July 13th, 1935

My dear Mrs. Thompson,

At a meeting of the Executive Committee of the Board of Trustees of the Library, held on July 11th, there was adopted a new budget, effective for the remainder of this fiscal year, that is, until Dec. 31st, 1935. Under the advice of the State Library Association's estimate for a wise budget, and taking into consideration the salary payments made by libraries similar to ours in service, it has been decided that the librarian should receive a monthly salary of $50.00. This change, the committee decided not to put into effect until the August payment, due on August 31st. Your cheque on July 31st will be for $70.00. . . . [The committee] also decided that the present page service be discontinued, and that the librarian be asked to assume the putting back of all books and cards. It is expected that the volunteer service now being done in cataloging and mending will so relieve the librarian as not to make this an extra burden. The allotment for books was put at $300.00 per year, considerably less than at present. . . . All these reductions are much to be deplored, and were adopted with regret and after full consideration of any ways in which they could have been avoided. It was, however, the unanimous opinion of the committee that only in adopting such a budget could we conscientiously administer the finances of the library.

With the appreciation on the part of the committee, and that of all the Trustees for your valuable services to the Library,

Very sincerely yours,
Julia S. Leaycraft
Secretary

Mrs. Thompson had always been careful about staying within the budget for books and she had hit upon a scheme that enabled her to buy many secondhand novels at bargain prices. During a visit to New York City she discovered that she could buy fiction culled from the rental shelf of the Channel Book Shop as "no longer in demand" for a fraction of their list price. In this way she was able, she said, "to keep our readers supplied with popular books" — to be sure, weeks or sometimes months old — nevertheless "best sellers" when first published.

Several members of the Book Committee protested against this practice, while others (including the librarian) felt that it was better to have *many* books rather than only a few straight off the press.

Before the end of July the State Library succeeded in locating for Woodstock a trained librarian on relief, a Mrs. Carol MacGahan who had served as a summer librarian at the Haines Falls library. And her memo, dated August 5, 1935 and signed with initials was addressed to Miss Doughty. Here it is in full:

There are approximately 4750 books now accessioned and on the shelves. Doubling this figure, as there are both an author card and a title card for each book, shows about 9500 cards (large) in the files.

The errors (including actual mistakes and markedly slovenly cards) run about 55%. That is to say, out of the 9500 cards in the files it will be necessary to replace about 5225 cards. Of these necessary replacements, 490 have already been done, leaving 4735 still to be done. We have, at present, approximately 150 cards left. I suggest ordering 5000 new catalogue cards.

N.B. These figures include no estimate of the cards necessary for new and newly accessioned books, which are coming to me rapidly at present.

The Executive Committee, meeting regularly once a month, continued to keep an eagle eye on expenses. It even questioned the library's need for a telephone, since it was "costing us two-fifty a month."

"Mrs. Thompson pleaded for its continuance," Mrs. Leaycraft wrote. "It was voted to keep it on another month, and have it listed under Mrs. Thompson's name after that, in order to avoid a higher business rate. Other needs were discussed. A typewriter is much needed. It was voted to have the Administration Committee look into the purchase of one, and report back.

"When the estimated cost of an oil-burning furnace ($600) was discussed Miss Webster said there were often six to ten inches of standing water in the cellar and the cost of deepening and pumping it would bring the total to at least a thousand dollars. Mr. Comeau pointed out that to go from three small stoves that seemed quite a jump and advocated our progressing more gradually."

All in all, it is scarcely surprising that "the request [by whom is not stated] that the Library be enlarged so as to make room for the Historical Society" got exactly nowhere.

Only five members of the Executive Committee were present when it met in November. Reports were read and motions made and seconded in jig time: "The Town Board has appropriated $100.00 for the Library this year, same as last. Mr. Purcell [who had succeeded Alice Owen as chairman of Administration] said he had learned that a made-over typewriter would cost at least $25.00. It was moved and passed that the Executive Committee cooperate with Administration to get one for less, if possible, and have someone try it before taking it."

21

The Brochure; "Donations, Please"

Of great interest to the trustees at this time (1935) was the newly-hatched plan to have Mr. Comeau and Mrs. Schoonmaker prepare a brochure to be sent out the following spring with the membership renewal notices: a printed bulletin "containing a full report of what the new library has been doing in the last few years."

So much had been accomplished in the immediate past, however, that the committee of two devoted much time and effort to the preparation of the preliminary draft. Later, Mrs. Schoonmaker reported that when the material for the bulletin had been submitted to several of the officers and board members for suggestions and corrections there was some diversity of opinion as to its contents, "with the result that most of these suggestions seem to have been gracefully ignored."

In its final form the bulletin started out bravely:

With every passing years THE WOODSTOCK LIBRARY establishes itself more firmly as one of the invaluable institutions of our little community. Its increasing membership, its extension service not only in the village but to all parts of the township, the aid it gives to school children, both grade and high, the successful effort it makes to serve the whole community, made up of such widely diversified interests — these are facts which are very well known to all who have acquainted themselves with what the Library is doing. . . .

The most impressive visible accomplishment of the immediate past is the alterations which have been made in the building itself.

At long last the library now had its "quiet reading room" — the Ell, no less. Soon after Miss Webster left in June, new shelving had been installed and the non-fiction moved — hence the name "the reference room." When describing the work on the card catalog the writers went all out:

But no single improvement equals in importance that of re-cataloguing the entire book stock. There are in the Library more than 6000 volumes; the old catalogue was incomplete and unsatisfactory. This labor of re-cataloguing has been a colossal one. The State Library, of which we are now a member, gave us the free services of a skilled librarian for several weeks. The actual work of typing, filing, etc. was done by volunteers. And no better evidence of the popular faith in the Library could have been given than by the response to this call for volunteer help. Men and women, young and old, artists and old Woodstockers gave days, even weeks, to this task.

Surely few libraries could boast of so many amateurs able to type and file correctly! Had the memo to Miss Doughty stating that more than 5000 cards would have to be replaced because of "mistakes and slovenly marked cards" been forgotten so soon?

The services which the Library offers to the community are varied.

Adult Department: We purchase, for adults, something like 250 volumes a year, maintaining a just balance between history, science, philosophy, economics, biography, fiction, drama, poetry, etc. In addition to these, we have given to us something like 300 volumes a year — another evidence of the popular appreciation of the Library. We seek always to improve our unusual collection of art books, pictures, etc., which are of great use to the established artists as well as to the art students who come in summer.

Junior Department: For this department we buy about 50 volumes annually and borrow 100 volumes a year from Albany. . . .

Extension Service: We are beginning to build up this service by which books are delivered to members who have no way of reaching the Library. Those who have received books in this way, in Willow, for instance, declare that their winters have been made a thousand-fold happier. It is satisfying to note that these readers ask for (and get) books on such varied topics as history, philosophy, science, higher mathematics, etc. It is hoped eventually to extend this service and send out a regular book truck over a much wider area. . . .

No more solid evidence of the growth and of the appreciation of the Library could be had than by comparing some of the actual figures. Taking the year 1930, for instance, we find that, operating on a budget of $1400, 5000 volumes passed out over the librarian's desk. This year, 1935, operating on a budget of $1200, 18,000 books have gone out. Since getting books out to readers is the first business of a library, that, surely, is a record to be proud of.

How could the library, operating on a budget of $1200 in 1935 do so much better than in 1930 with a budget $200 higher?

Possibly this was another correction "gracefully ignored." In 1930 the budget was actually $1,100. To this had been added $300 for "depreciation" but thereafter omitted as unnecessary.

How do we stretch a budget of $1200 over all these activities? And how do we get that same $1200?

The Library is not and never has been endowed.

Our money comes from three main sources: membership dues, special gifts or grants, and from various entertainments. The membership dues average between $450 and $500 a year, these memberships ranging in denomination from $25 to $1. Our annual summer Fair brings us between $500 and $600. The State Library gives us, as a member, an annual grant of $100 which must be spent for books.

The Woodstock Town Board has, for the last two years, given us from the town funds the sum of $100. For special needs and purposes we resort to special entertainments, a concert, a series of talks, book review evenings, etc., etc.

Only one item of this budget is fixed and guaranteed from year to year. Life for the Library is, therefore, precarious. Let the membership drop a bit or bad weather come to the Fair and a deficit will have to be faced. These are real problems which the Board of Trustees cannot escape. . . .

We look forward to the time when the Town Board may feel that an organization so vital to the life of our village deserves a larger apportionment from the town funds. Other libraries in other near-by towns receive much larger proportional amounts. Why should we not have ours lifted also?

Like a refrain those words "Why should we not have ours lifted also?" would be repeated again and again during the years to come.

A thousand of the eight-page brochures were printed and laboriously fastened together by the mending committee — two thousand thrusts of needles and thread, then a knot tied and a snip of the scissors. How those trustees worked!

"This has saved us considerable expense," Mrs. Schoonmaker said. "Copies were sent to all present and past members and to others such as officers of local organizations, ministers, leading citizens, members of the Town Board, trustees of all town schools and to such others who we thought might be interested in the work of the library.

"The returns from this little piece of strategy have been most gratifying even beyond what we dared hope for. Besides doubling or increasing their own subscriptions, many of the members added subscriptions for others in their family. And along with the checks, in many cases, came little notes. One lady wrote 'Here is my spring hat, I will wear my old one.' Another said, 'Here is my mite. I wish it were mightier.' One brother of a twenty-five dollar member sent his check for twenty-five dollars marked 'For the special use of the Book Committee.'

"It would not seem too foolish," Mrs. Schoonmaker added,

"to cherish the giddy hope that even the Town Board may eventually be convinced that we have a little institution worthy of far more financial support than that body is at present giving us."

22

A Highly Satisfactory Rating

Now in its tenth year in its own quarters, the Woodstock Library had reached what might be called a plateau in its affairs. By taking over the Ell after Miss Webster had left, much space had been gained: one room for the children; the other for the growing collection of non-fiction. This was all to the good; nevertheless, there was no blinking the fact that running expenses had been increased and that the Town Board, having upped its contribution from $50 to $100, had no intention of giving the library more.

At the meeting in June of 1936 the chairman of Finance, Martin Comeau, introduced the subject by saying that "every effort" should be made to obtain a larger contribution from the town. President Zimm was in complete agreement. "Take New Paltz for example," he said, "there's a town with approximately the same population as Woodstock, yet it gives its library a thousand dollars a year!"

The minutes note that after considerable discussion and comparison of "our service with other libraries, it was concluded that $500 would be a fair amount for Woodstock." But it was one thing to reach a decision on what would be a "fair amount" and quite another to follow the matter up with the Town Board. There is no record of further action.

Each year, well before the annual meeting, it was the custom hopefully to urge the same officers and committeemen to serve for another term. And numbers of them did; their names keep reappearing in the minutes time and again. Others, however, much preferred to step down and President Zimm was one of these. In her report, Miss Wardwell, chairman of the Nominating Committee, said that it was "with considerable difficulty" that she had persuaded Mr. Zimm to accept reelection. She, herself, had already taken on (and not for the first time) the job of Fair Chairman.

Intent on making the Country Fair that summer the most colorful and gay event of the season, Miss Wardwell asked her helpers, those in charge of booths and tables, to come decked out in bright costumes. They did, of course, and so did a surprising number of local people. As for the weather, it couldn't have been better if it had been made to order. And never before had the artists given so freely of their time and work. John Striebel offered to do portrait sketches for the benefit of the library and the list of those who had donated drawings to be raffled off included Konrad Cramer, Neil Ives, Orville Peets, Arnold Wiltz, Bradley Tomlin, Frank London, and Charles Rosen.

When the returns were in and every penny accounted for, the treasurer, Mr. Elwyn, was able to report at the meeting in August: "Receipts from Fair, $819.37; Expenses, posters, $10; cream, tables, moving [from wherever equipment had been temporarily stored], $14.25. Net profit, $775.22" — a tidy sum indeed.

Beginning in 1934 Mrs. Thompson received from headquarters in Albany a form headed *Library Efficiency Record.* This was the measuring stick by which the standing of a library, as compared with other libraries of similar size and importance, could be judged. Filled out in Albany and based on the librarian's annual report on circulation, stock, etc., the rating was bewilderingly complicated.*

Here is an abridged sample:

* The rating was based on the ratio between the standard and the record of the library, as determined by the use of the multiplication factor.

Book stock
Volumes per capita, credits 5, standard 5
     librarian's report 13.01
     multiplication factor 1
     rating in points 13.01
Volumes added per capita, credits 5, standard .25
     rating in points 24
Per cent children's books, credits 5, standard 25
     rating in points 3.62
Circulation per capita of population, credits, 5, standard 9
     rating in points 17.41
Finance, income per capita, credits 5, standard $1.00
     rating in points 16.75
     Expenditure per capita, credits 5, standard
      $1.00
     rating in points 12.10
     Tax per capita, credits 5, standard $.50
     rating in points 0.61

The number of volumes added per capita rating of 24 was considered very good, but per cent children's books rating, only 3.62, was poor and as for tax per capita rating of 0.61 it was so low as to be almost non-existent. There were 17 categories in all. Under "chief librarian, general education" there was a 5-point credit for four years of high school (all that was required) plus two additional points for Mrs. Thompson's two years of college. In 1937 the total rating added up to 189.67 which was exceptionally good since a total of 100 was "highly satisfactory." *

The trustees were elated, so was Mrs. Thompson. For her, the library was her life. She arrived early in the morning, left late in the afternoon, and at home put in endless hours of overtime preparing reports.

Open every day during the summer, except Sundays and

---

* The report dated 1946 has a note added in red ink longhand: "Your library ranked *3rd* of *81* libraries in its class."

Mondays, from two until six and also on Saturday morning from eleven until one in the afternoon, the hours were long for one librarian and her two now-and-then assistants. She received $600 a year and the helpers were paid, between them, a total of $80.10 figured at twenty-five cents an hour.

This small "above average" library was still heated with stoves, it still lacked an indoor toilet, and certain patrons did not hesitate to complain about that "smelly place out back." Every Halloween the village boys banded together at night and tipped the old privy over on its side, and every year the library had to hire men to hoist it back on its shaky foundation, adding a few extra nails in the hope that "next time it won't go over." But it did — many a next time.

On the last page of the minutes for December, under the heading New Business, comes the following: "The President announced that the Historical Society has asked us, together with other organizations of the town, to send a representative to the meeting to be held on Jan. 11 to organize a celebration of the town's sesquicentennial celebration which will be celebrated next summer. The Board appointed Mrs. Schoonmaker to represent us."

23

The Stone from Blenheim Palace

One Thursday evening in April of 1937 several members of the Central Celebration Committee met in the library to work on the booklet-program for the coming Woodstock Sesquicentennial. Their names are not a matter of record, but the 35-page booklet is still available. It opens with a historical sketch of how Woodstock came into being: "On a day in spring, one hundred and fifty years ago this year, a little band of white men met together in this valley to give legal form to the government of a township. . . ."

From the purchase of an enormous stretch of land from the Indians, the story traces the development of the wilderness and the Woodstock of 1770 to the modern Woodstock of 1937. One name mentioned along the way is that of Ralph Radcliffe Whitehead of Byrdcliffe, followed by a short account of his search for an ideal place to establish an arts and crafts colony. But nowhere is there any reference to the Woodstock Library. Yet "the weekly Market Fair, the summer theater and a winter sports association" were given several lines.

We do not know who first proposed writing to Woodstock, Oxford, England about its one-hundred-fifty-year-old daughter in Ulster County, New York. Like as not it was Mrs. Bruno Zimm, President of the Historical Society, since the reply — a cablegram signed Cyril Morris, Mayor — was addressed to her: "Hearty congratulations on your celebration from Woodstock."

This was followed by a letter to Mrs. Zimm from Stanley Henman: "I am directed by the Mayor and the Corporation of Woodstock, England to inform you that we are sending out to you a stone from Blenheim Palace, Woodstock, to be built into the war memorial which you are erecting. The size of this stone is 2 feet long by 1 foot high and 6 inches deep. A suitable inscription will be made on the stone, which will be forwarded to you as quickly as possible. I will write you further in due course."

Here was a news item of interest to all the readers of the *Kingston Daily Freeman.* Under the heading "Blenheim Stone, All Blessed, Inscribed, Sails to Woodstock," is the following:

Woodstock, May 27, 1937. — The faithful Stanley Henman, town clerk of Woodstock, in Oxford, England, writes again to Mrs. Bruno Zimm, on paper embossed with the seal of the borough:

Dear Madam —

Further to my letter to you of the 22nd April last I have pleasure in informing you that the stone referred to in my previous letter has been completed and is being dispatched to you forthwith. The stone bears the following inscription:

1787–1937

to

WOODSTOCK, NEW YORK

In kindred sympathy and peaceful
association this stone from
Blenheim Palace
is dedicated

by

WOODSTOCK, ENGLAND
In the Year of the Coronation of
H. M. King George VI.

It was dedicated by the Rector of Woodstock on Coronation Day, and is presented by the Mayor, Alderman and Burgesses of the Borough of Woodstock with good will and in the earnest hope that the friendship existing between the two towns and countries will continue and mature in the bonds of everlasting peace.

Yours faithfully,
STANLEY HENMAN,
Town Clerk's Office
Woodstock, England.

As might be expected, the published letter sparked a search for information about the famous palace. Was it still standing?

It was, indeed. Moreover, an illustrated official guide, published in England, was available. From it one learned that Blenheim Palace covers nearly three acres of ground and that there are necessarily hundreds of chimneys but "the architect had cleverly obscured every one!" And while the palace is no longer open to the public, the visitor (for a modest fee) could view the gardens "gloriously ablaze with richly colored blooms in summer."

The guide also states, "The place-name is of Saxon origin, derived from *Vudestoc,* denoting a stockaded settlement in a wood. . . . In the Domesday Book (1086) Woodstock appears as *Wodestock* and is described as a royal forest."

In due time "the birthday stone" arrived and proved to be a fairly heavy block of limestone, yellowish in color, bearing the beautifully inscribed message to Woodstock, N.Y.

The Historical Society, however, was at a loss to know what to do with it for the original plan to incorporate it in the war memorial on the village green was no longer possible now that the design for the memorial had been changed. It may have been Mrs. Zimm herself who proposed offering the stone to the library. The trustees accepted it with thanks and after much puzzling decided to store it in the no longer used fireplace, carefully tilted at an angle so that the inscription could be read. And there it would remain for the next eleven years.

24

A Well Advertised Fair; A Close Call

Each year as the library's book collection continued to outgrow the limited shelf space, one or another of the trustees wondered aloud what, if anything, could be done to enlarge the building. The annual Country Fairs, too, continued to increase in size and importance and this was due in large part to the way the publicity was handled.

In 1938 Norman T. Boggs, reporting for the Publicity Committee, said that four weeks before the Fair scheduled for Wednesday July 28, he began to mail out stories about the Fair's fun and fantastic bargains to all daily and weekly papers within a radius of fifty miles. Posters were sent to outlying inns and teahouses and to at least ten libraries known to be interested in the Fair. More than 2000 handbills, just the right size to fit theater programs, were printed and distributed. One local newspaper, *The Overlook*, devoted so much space to the coming Fair, listing everyone who presided over a table, together with the names of their helpers, that the account reads like a who's who of Woodstock:

Women's and men's clothing will again be an important feature, the former in charger of Mrs. James T. Shotwell and Mrs. Doris U. Fleming; the latter in charge of Mrs. Norman T. Boggs. No table at the Fair produces larger returns than that of women's clothing. Friends of the Library are, therefore, urged to send in misfits, discarded or unbecoming garments which may be sold for the good cause. . . . Mrs. Griffin Herrick, who has served as flower chairman almost since the Fair was instituted, has assisting her this year Miss Anita Smith of Stonecrop Gardens and Miss Alice Henderson. . . .

The toys presided over this year by Mrs. Walter Weyl, together with her committee, Mrs. Walter O'Meara, Mrs. Alfred Jones, Mrs. Nathaniel Weyl and Miss Bollman will include a group of Mexican toys brought back especially for the Fair by Mrs. Weyl who went tripping to Mexico last winter.

The lack of a collection center of any kind greatly added to the difficulty of managing a fair and this was brought home in a report signed Julia Leaycraft, chairman: "There were so many clothes left over that they were hung in Mrs. Peets's studio for several days and further sales made. The heads of the Red Cross, Dutch Church and the Women's Auxiliary of the Legion were asked to come at a specified time and pick out what was needed for the town, or for sending to refugees. After that, the remaining things were taken to the Salvation Army in Kingston. Before the final wind-up, a boxful of silk clothing was picked out for use another year, and this is stored in the Peets's studio. I would suggest a still larger selling force. . . . There is such a press of people about the booth that three more could be used. I advise small prices and try to get rid of everything. Very few things sell for over two dollars. Better to price things at 50 cts. or even a quarter and get the money."

That year, 1940, the Women's Clothing Booth made $177.84 and the total net receipts were $1072.20.

The Book Committee was still meeting regularly once a month but no longer in the library. Now the meetings were being held in private homes, with the hostess serving refreshments. Claire Friedberg was the chairman and her first report, delivered at the trustees' meeting in September of 1940, put the facts in a nutshell:

"The July meeting was held at the home of one of our members, Mrs. Judson Phillips, where Mr. Nathaniel Weyl was our guest speaker. The August meeting was held at Dr. James T. Shotwell's home. Alfred Kreyemborg spoke. At our summer meetings we invited members of the committee of former years and relaxed while we listened to others talk. But during the other months we earnestly try to proportion our money wisely according to the needs and wishes of the public."

One newspaper that made a practice of devoting a generous amount of space to library matters was the *Ulster County News,* and in its issue of June 18, 1942 the annual meeting rated a double column headline: "Isabel Doughty Re-elected Library President Last Week."

The trustees, it seems, had refused to accept her resignation and she was re-elected by a standing vote. After listing the names of the other officers, committee chairmen, and trustees elected for a three-year term, the story continues: "The treasurer's report showed that the library had stayed well within its budget. All seven school districts contributed a total of $150, the town of Woodstock $200. . . . Mrs. Alice Thompson, librarian, reported additional books during the year bringing the total up to 11,173. Fewer are in circulation because of war activities and departure of men in service. . . ."

All but a few of the minutes and reports by committeemen during this period are missing, but we do have carbons of two letters signed by President Doughty. One is addressed to Mr. Mervin J. Doremus, the other to Miss Helen Jones. Both are dated March 29, 1941; the wording is identical.

"Dear Miss Jones" (the one to the Library's janitor begins), "Following up my informal expression of gratitude to you at the time, I wish to thank you formally in behalf of the reading public in general and the Board of Trustees of the Library in particular for your prompt action in preventing what might have been a disastrous fire. Although the Library and contents are insured, there are many books which could never be replaced. We all owe you a great deal and we want you to know that we are deeply appreciative."

Helen Jones is blessed with an excellent memory. "It must have happened after midnight," she told us. "I'd been asleep quite a while when the phone rang. Mr. Doremus knew I had a key to the Library. He said, 'Get down there as fast as you can and check on the stoves.' I don't live far, you know, and it didn't take me long to get some clothes on and get there. He was waiting for me. As soon as I got the front door open we both went in — but only as far as the *door* to the back room of the Ell where the stove was. It was red hot and jumping up and down! The woodwork was all charred and the paint blistered. It was so hot in the room we couldn't even go in long enough to shut off the stove. So I ran around outside to where the oil tank was and turned off the valve in the feed pipe. As soon as the oil in the line was used up the fire went out of course — lucky thing, too, that old frame house would have burned like match wood.

"Probably what happened," she went on, "is that when it was time to close the library somebody turned the stove *up* by mistake instead of turning it down." When asked how Mr. Doremus had discovered that the stove was overheating Miss Jones said, "He told me he had smelled oil. I think he was on his way home, on Library Lane, passing right by the library."

It was indeed a close call and reason enough, it would seem, to revive the long-discussed plan to do away with the stoves and install a furnace — but not while the country was at war. "Ulster County aims to sell enough bonds to purchase an ambulance plane," the members of the library were told, "and while your contributions are actually gifts, the War Bond they buy for the library is a savings investment."

Once again the members rose to the occasion and a War Bond for $370 became part of the library's assets.

25

Warplane Spotters

The artists and other members of the library did far more than contribute money toward its purchase of the War Bond. For example, when the Woodstock Observation Post for the Aircraft Warning Service was erected on Anita Smith's property in Rock City in 1942, she was appointed Chief Observer under the U.S. Army Airforce First Fighter command.

Classes were held regularly in the Town Hall. All "spotters" were expected to memorize the body and wing structure — as seen from below — of airplanes that might appear over the valley; then, if one were seen, to report instantly, via telephone, to the Filter Board in New York City.

The Observation Post had been built with lumber and other materials donated by patriotic citizens. It consisted of a small house surrounded by a platform mounted on tall posts. To reach it a spotter had to climb a long flight of wooden steps.

In her entertaining book, *Woodstock: History and Hearsay,* Miss Smith tells the story of the Observation Post. By 1942, she says:

there were over a hundred observers [working two-hour shifts at a time around the clock] . . . and it took real stamina to man the Post throughout the winter. One night the temperature dropped to 32 degrees below zero with a gale blowing, yet the listening window was never closed. The little stove puffed valiantly and showers of blessings fell on those kind friends, who, unable to serve themselves, gave fuel. . . .

The second winter there were stove troubles. It was difficult for the old timers to realize the present generation did not know how to keep a wood stove going.

One old-timer remembers, too, peering anxiously through field glasses at a high-flying plane and hoping she was correct when reporting by phone that she'd just seen a Boeing B17, Flying Fortress.

On October 4, 1943, more than a year before the war ended in May of 1945, Chief Observer Anita Smith was notified that the work of the Ground Observer Corps was being curtailed. In other words, the Woodstock Post was no longer needed. It had, however, chalked up an impressive record. Among those who received medals for having served over 250 hours on the Post were Isabel Doughty, Julia Leaycraft, and Konrad Cramer. But top honors went to the Chief Observer herself: Anita Smith was credited with over 1200 hours.

Those who attended the movies in the Town Hall during the war years had reason to remember the effect that rationing of fuel oil had on the temperature of the hall. Never above 50 degrees, the place was so cold that many in the audience sat bundled to the ears in winter coats and with blankets wrapped around their knees.

At last the war ended, summer came once more, and with it, the annual Fair. Held in July, as was now established custom, the 1946 event was an outstanding success with its net profit of $4,025.85. The clothing department turned in $485.23 with the jewelry table doing almost as well, $439.43. That year Walter Van Wagenen, principal of the Woodstock School, served as both handy man and treasurer. During a recent interview he spoke of the "horrendous task" of carting all the Fair equipment down from Ben Webster's place in Byrdcliffe. "That's where it had been stored for the winter," he said, "but I didn't mind that as much as I did having to guard more than four thousand dollars in cash overnight. You see, Woodstock had no bank in those days so there was nothing for it but to take the money home with me and sit up with it. Then next morning Clancy, our policeman, and I drove to Kingston and put the money in the library's savings account."

26

The New Wing and a Drive for Funds

The growing sense of confidence in the Fairs as money-makers was bound to set one trustee in particular to toying with the idea of enlarging the library.

When making her report as chairman of the Fair Committee, Katherine Boyd said, "Many of us believe we should begin as soon as possible to make plans for a new building. However, when speaking of a 'new' library I do not necessarily mean tearing down this old one — it might be incorporated in the new part. And my reason for bringing this to the attention of the Board now is two-fold. First, the need is obvious and was stressed by Miss Ridgeway, the inspector from Albany, and second, the psychological effect on the public. It would answer the question so many ask: 'What are you going to do with this money you make at the Fair?' "

Mrs. Boyd had been impressed by the fine photographs taken during the Fair by Helen Shotwell. These she was giving to the library "so that all monies collected from the sale of the pictures could be set aside toward a prize for the best design by our local architects for our new library." Mrs. Boyd concluded by saying she felt this would arouse a great deal of public interest and I have no doubt "would bring in some sizeable sums."

Any plan to enlarge the library was of particular interest to Frances Rogers, a trustee and chairman of the Book Committee since 1943. But when month after month slipped by with nothing whatever being done about the proposed prize, she decided to do a little quiet investigating on her own. At the executive meeting in August of 1947 she said, "I believe there is ample space right back of the library for a good-sized addition. I've measured it. We could have a wing at least fifty feet long. One tree would have to come down, but the tool shed and the Ladies-and-Gents could stay where it is. . . ."

George Neher, the president, and Walter Van Wagenen, still serving as treasurer, welcomed the proposal. They saw no point, they said, in wasting time and money on a prize. Far better to choose the right architect and have him draw up the plans.

At a special meeting of the board called by Mr. Neher, the plan to add a room at the back of the library was discussed in great detail. And when someone suggested that Albert Graeser, the architect who designed the Town Hall, built in 1936–37, would be the very man for the job, this was followed by a vote to ask Mr. Graeser to look the building over and see what he thought about enlarging the library in that way.

After inspecting the place in front and back, and the interior from the wet cellar to the roof, the architect reported that he considered the proposal to add a room along the back wall a good one, but while the trustees were at it, why not extend the new structure around the corner, so to speak? By replacing part of the Ell it would be possible to increase the size of the children's room, and between it and the front office there would be space for a small but adequate toilet for the staff. Then in order to install a furnace it would be necessary to construct a deep, waterproof room in the cellar.

At the board's request the architect would make the wing "as fireproof as possible." So, in his preliminary drawing the concrete block addition — 54 x 20 feet — was equipped with steel doors in the opening between the new part and the old building, doors that could be rolled back during library hours. The room should indeed be fireproof. An entry in the October minutes reads: "Albert Graeser $25 — initial payment on architect's fee."

The next step was to get the State Library's approval of the layout. After an exchange of letters Marion Moshier * arrived. She was eminently fitted to pass judgment and she spotted the errors immediately, pointing out that no part of a library should be closed off to make it fireproof. "Libraries seldom burn," she said. "What you must do is to have a wide opening here — no doors — a wide arch here above low book shelves and here," she indicated the wall between the Ell and the main room. "You've allotted too much space to the office. Leave it as it is now and increase the size of the children's room by just that much more. In short, keep everything as open as possible so the librarian can see into the other rooms from her desk in this room."

Before leaving, Miss Moshier said that she was amazed that a library with a circulation close to 20,000 could operate on a budget of little over $3,000 and in "such inadequate space."

As soon as the revised plan had been approved by the State Library, the architect completed his working drawings and blueprints were sent to several local contractors for bids.

It was now mid-winter and because of personal reasons President Neher regretfully resigned and Walter Van Wagenen was elected to succeed him, with Herbert Wyman taking over as treasurer. When the executive committee met to open the sealed bids, the ones submitted by Frank Bradley, general contractor, and Adolph Heckerorth, for plumbing, heating and wiring, proved to be the lowest. They were accepted by unanimous vote but it took far longer to figure out how much the library could safely invest in the project and how much would have to be raised through a drive for funds. After a decision had been reached, a printed letter, dated February 1948, was mailed to the membership.

To the Members of the Woodstock Library
The Board of Trustees has asked me to write you that we are

* Co-author with Helena LeFever of *The Small Public Library*.

planning to renovate the present building, and put on an addition . . . after careful investigation [we have] decided to put $8000 of our resources into a building fund. The annual budget of the Library is now $3,200 and since the Library Fair has recently been very successful, even though we have a constantly rising budget, the Trustees felt the sum of $8000 could safely be invested in the building. . . . In spite of the present high costs, it was felt by the Trustees that we delay no longer. All reports indicate that there is no prospect of reduction in price of building materials.

The trustees considered tearing down the present building, but the additional cost would be prohibitive, and the majority wanted to preserve the charm of the old building.

On opening the bids for the construction, it was found that the total cost of the addition and renovation will be $20,000. This means that there will be $12,000 to be raised in addition to the $8,000 allotted by the Library.

A special fund raising committee has been appointed, with Rev. Harvey Todd as chairman, and later the whole community will be approached through this committee.

The plans are at the Library for any member to see. They include a fine children's room, a heating system, and plumbing. The interior will be opened up to provide a reading room, and the addition for the first time will provide adequate housing for our special collections of music and art.

This letter is a report to the members, who are, of course, the group from whom the President and Board of Trustees are elected, and whose approval and support are counted on to back this plan. This is not an appeal for money at this time.

Walter Van Wagenen, President

So important was Mr. Todd's fund raising committee to the success of the project that the members were chosen with care: Sidney Berkowitz, treasurer and publicity; Morris Klein, secretary; Walter Van Wagenen (ex officio); Alf Evers, and Mrs. Weyl. Later, other names were added to the list, but very few of the official members of this committee were expected to attend the many meetings held in

March and April. Here is an excerpt from the minutes of one such meeting dated March 20:

"April 30th (Friday) was suggested for cornerstone laying, with the campaign to begin next day, May 1st. Trustees are asked to decide what should be placed in cornerstone. A good many guests are to be invited [to the dinner for the workers to be paid for by an anonymous donor] and lists of workers should be ready. Mr. Berkowitz is arranging with *The Sunday News* for a full page ad at the beginning of the campaign. This will not cost the committee anything. The seven campaign zones were studied and captains suggested for all of them. Mr. Todd reported that Mr. [Paul] Arndt suggested asking artists to donate good pictures. Mr. Arndt was suggested as chairman."

Mr. Todd's committee was determined to make the most of every opportunity to keep the community's interest in the library's need for funds at high pitch and arrangements were made to attract a crowd the day ground was broken for the new wing. The well-advertised event was scheduled to begin at four in the afternoon of March 3, and although the architect who was expected momentarily had not arrived, Mr. Van Wagenen decided that it was much too cold and windy to delay the ceremony more than a few minutes. So he swung a vigorous pick into the frozen ground in line with the old building and Grand Elwyn, town clerk, removed the first shovelful of earth to the cheers of some forty spectators. Then, just in time to join those trooping into the Town Hall to see the beautiful little model of the completed library building, Mr. Graeser arrived somewhat out of breath. His car had been stuck in a snowbank near his home on Ohayo Mountain, he said, and he had had to shovel it out.

Before an audience of more than a hundred interested citizens the little model was unveiled by the architect who explained the plan for enlarging the library, after which Mr. Van Wagenen and Mr. Todd spoke at length. Mr. Elwyn delivered a message from the Town Board: "The Town

Board assures you that they are in complete accord with all your aims and desires."

Particularly welcome that cold day must have been the coffee and doughnuts served by Mrs. Lindin and Miss Elsa Kimball and their committee.

27

The Laying of the Cornerstone; Open House

Work on the new wing proceeded smoothly and everything was in readiness for the next publicized event — the laying of the cornerstone on April 30th. That the cornerstone would be the limestone block from Woodstock, England, was generally known but what was indeed news was that the trowel had also come from England where it had been used in 1858 for the cornerstone laying of a Memorial School in Willington Quay.

Despite an occasional light spring shower, the ceremony was conducted without interruption with clergymen from each of the local churches taking turns in handling the trowel. And because the stone was solid, the articles supposed to go into the cornerstone were placed in the three hollow sections of the concrete building block upon which it would rest.

Stationed next to the waist-high foundation, Claire Friedberg described each article as she placed it in the block: a letter signed by President Van Wagenen; a newspaper; and a picture of the Library Fair painted by Helen Shotwell. Then, seemingly in response to a sudden impulse, she beckoned to a young boy. "Please come here, Bill. Let's see what you have in your pocket — what a boy of today carries about with him should be of future interest too."

As Bill handed over a collection of odds and ends — a pocket knife, string, marbles, and so on — the crowd, amused, laughed and applauded. The person standing next to Georgina Klitgaard, however, heard her mutter; "That's too smooth — it looks planned." Well, it was. But only Mrs.

Friedberg, Frances Rogers, the chairman of the Building Committee, Bill and his mother, Mrs. Heckeroth, knew about it in advance. Unimportant? Of course, but calculated to give the spectators something to talk about later. Anything that would remind the community of the library and its drive for funds was all to the good.

The incident even made the papers, but it was the two-column headline in one local newspaper that caught the eye: "Senator Wicks Raps Reds and Nazis at Woodstock Library." At first glance it seemed to imply that the library was harboring Reds and Nazis! But the accompanying article set the record straight: "In the course of his speech at Town Hall, following the outdoor ceremony, the Senator, hitting at the Nazi and Communistic ideologies, stressed the American way of life and declared, 'Thank God here in America the soul of an artist is his own.' "

Before leaving Woodstock, Senator Wicks gave $50 to the library's building fund.

Much to the surprise of many of the trustees, contributions to the fund lagged far behind expectations. At the annual meeting in June the treasurer reported that 476 donors had given a total of $4,524 with $1001.50 more in pledges — a disappointingly low sum. Later, at a meeting held at Mr. Todd's, the building fund committee discussed ways in which to raise money. Mr. Berkowitz offered to run a movie at the Art Gallery between two art exhibitions, and Mr. Todd said he would find out whether a musicale at the home of Mrs. Lindin might be arranged. "It was decided to attempt a vaudeville show right after the season at the Playhouse," Secretary Klein wrote. "Volunteer talent and no rental charge by the theater would enable us to make an easy profit. A special committee is to be appointed."

The annual Fair, scheduled this time for Thursday August 5, had long since shed its original name "Country Fair," and no one questioned the announcement that it would be the 21st consecutive Library Fair. Actually it was 16th, since the first one held on Mr. Lasher's big field in front of the library took place in 1931, not in 1927, the date used in the reckoning. Prior to the first Country Fair, the library's money-raising events were known as bazaars, rummage sales, or white elephant sales, never as Library Fairs.

Thursday morning the sky was bright without a cloud to mask the sun, but as the day wore on and the heat increased there was talk of the likelihood of a thunderstorm. Luckily, it did not rain and during the four hours in the afternoon, $3,252.45 was taken in.

That year Walter Van Wagenen, in addition to being president, served as Fair Finance chairman and he recalls how busy he, together with Herbert Wyman, George Neher, and two others were kept while counting and double-checking the piles of bills and quantity of change — all by hand — while keeping track of the amount credited to each department for money received.

A newspaper published locally, *Woodstock Weekly Window* (August 5, 1948), ran an editorial headed "And the End Is Not Yet."

Those who are active in Woodstock . . . and who isn't . . . are beginning to feel the strain of the hectic pace being set by a multitude of summer activities. One after another of the traditional events pass by in the fast moving procession and as each one is completed, those who staged it or worked in it or attended it, mop their fevered brows and brace themselves for the next one. Like the man on the treadmill, they cannot stop.

The program for this summer is more crowded than usual. There are more theatrical programs, more concerts, more art exhibitions, more lectures, and more everything than in previous years. . . .

Would this explain, in part, why the Library Building Fund was still so far below its goal of $12,000?

All the minutes covering the regular meetings of the Executive Committee and the board during this period have disappeared. We do have, however, Herbert Wyman's Treasurer's report given at the annual meeting in June of 1949 with a summary of the amounts paid the architect and the contractors since the addition had been completed in November 1948, and the balance still due them. Here is the way he presented the statement in longhand:

	Graeser	*Bradley*	*Heckeroth*
Contract Price	$ 1,154.21	$16,158.62	$3,078.29
Amount Paid	953.59	15,365.00	2,650.90
Balance Due	200.62	793.00	427.39
Total Cost	$20,391.12		
Total Paid	18,969.49		
Balance Due	$ 1,421.63		

The Building Fund Committee had turned in $6331.91; consequently, instead of the $8000 the trustees had allocated to the project, they were faced with supplying $14,059.21. Again we learn from the treasurer's report how this was managed: "Bank Loan $1000; War Bond $370 plus interest $41.67" and the rest from the savings account which reduced it to less than $2000 on hand for running expenses. Nevertheless, twenty-one years after the Woodstock Club's first reception to celebrate the opening of the Library in its new quarters, the Lasher House, attended by fifty persons, the newly enlarged Woodstock Library's "Open House," held on Friday, November 26, 1948, entertained two hundred guests. Refreshments were served by a committee composed of trustees. The speaker, Dr. James T. Shotwell, was introduced by President Walter Van Wagenen.

The following summer the annual Fair, counted as a great success, racked up a total of $3,754.52, thus enabling the library to begin to mend its financial fences.

PART THREE : 1951-1959

28

The Charter; A Patch of Thin Ice

The provisional charter had been renewed twice and now, in 1951, rather than apply for a further extension the trustees decided to try for an absolute charter. The application blank supplied by the State Library called for detailed information which President Morris Klein filled in by hand. For example:

Bound books in good condition	17,606
Estimated value	$9,755
Books needing repair	117
Estimated value	$50
Other property, cases & furniture	$1,000
Building & land	$26,000
Cash on hand	$4,800
Hours open	Four hours on four days of the week and two hours in addition on Saturday mornings
Salary of librarian	$1,200
Salary of assistants	$820

Then followed other questions about fines and postage.

The Town Board was contributing $600 and Mr. Klein wrote in one of the blank spaces: "We understand the town would grant us additional funds when the Fair did not raise enough for our budget." He then added the following:

Proceeds of Annual Fair

1941	$1,312.83	1946	$4,025.52
1942	1,641.95	1947	3,517.71
1943	1,467.44	1948	3,280.95
1944	2,154.69	1949	3,423.88
1945	2,838.76	1950	3,730.05

Much to everyone's gratification the Board of Regents granted the charter and when the official-looking document arrived the trustees had it framed and placed on the wall behind the librarian's desk.

Mrs. Thompson had set something of a record for long and devoted service. Starting in the fall of 1927 as "winter assistant" to Edith Macomb, Alice Thompson had been checking books in and out for nearly twenty-four years and the exacting work was beginning to take its toll. When overtired or exasperated for one reason or another, she was frequently heard to exclaim, "This is too much, I'm going to resign!" No one, however, took her seriously. But it so happened that during a meeting of the Book Committee in the summer of 1951, Lynn Wells, who was present as a guest because she cared about books and had recently purchased property in Woodstock, pricked up her ears when she heard Mrs. Thompson say to no one in particular as she gathered up her papers, "This is enough to make me resign!"

"Resign?" The very word gave Mrs. Wells food for thought. A few weeks later she asked one of the trustees if Mrs. Thompson's daughter, Betty, would automatically inherit her mother's job as librarian when she retired.

That possibility had never been discussed by the board. Betty Thompson Schrader was a very capable assistant but she did not have the technical training currently expected of librarians in charge of even small chartered libraries. And this, most likely, was what Mrs. Wells was told. In September she returned to New Brunswick, N.J., to resume the position she had held for many years: principal of Rutgers Elementary School.

It may seem odd now that one or more of those reasonable trustees did not think ahead and question what should be done about the elderly librarian when she did, in fact, retire. They were aware that she was already past seventy, the age of retirement recommended by the State Library. They were also aware that the library had no pension plan; its own financial future was too uncertain. The town's contribution of $600 fell far short of the budget (in 1951, $3,821) and its annual Fair, its mainstay, was at best a gamble at the mercy of the weather. Possibly one reason the subject of her retirement had been allowed to slide was in line with the old adage about not missing the water till the well runs dry. As long as Mrs. Thompson was at her desk there was water in the proverbial well.

At the close of the school year, in the spring of 1952, Mrs. Wells, as was her custom, returned to her summer home in Woodstock. Having resigned as principal of the elementary school, she planned to become a permanent resident of Woodstock, so she let it be known that strictly *on her own* she had taken a course in Library Science during the winter and that *if* and *when* the post of librarian became vacant she would like to file an application.

Here appeared to be an unexpected solution to a problem that would have to be faced sooner or later. Certainly Mrs. Thompson could not be expected to continue much longer and the prospect of finding a replacement — a qualified person willing to take a part-time job at small pay — should be given serious consideration.

On June 19, in order to discuss the subject "informally," the Executive Committee met at Miss Wardwell's house on Glasco Turnpike. Those present that Sunday afternoon were the two honorary trustees, Miss Wardwell and Mrs. Weyl, Ex-President Klein and his successor Houston Richards, Vice-President Rose Oxhandler, Miss Rogers, Miss Doughty, Mr.

Wetterau, Chairman of Finance, Secretary Pauline Summers, and Jane (Mrs. William) Shirey, chairman of the Book Committee.

They had all read the outline of Educational qualifications submitted by Mrs. Wells, a college graduate. Furthermore, she was a friendly, outgoing sort of person with much executive experience who was willing, she had said, to work for whatever salary was currently being paid by the library.

"Before discussing the *future* needs of the library," Mr. Klein proposed, "we should take a good hard look at the special conditions under which this particular library must operate."

"I think we can all agree to that," Mr. Wetterau responded, "but it should not be the sort of memorandum one jots down on the back of an old envelope."

The entry in the minutes appears as follows:

"1: So many people who are interested in the Library are either away a good deal — or cannot give the time they would like to because of the pressure of other responsibilities.

"2: The financing of the Library being chiefly dependent on the Library Fair, is a more and more heavy undertaking.

"3: Our ability to offer only a part-time position, in the country, with small pay.

"4: And most important, the need — (which has, happily, been met up to now by Mrs. Thompson's unusual and devoted service) — the need for a librarian who will have a very personal interest in the community and the Library, and hence give it much more thought and time and energy than we have any right to expect."

So far, so good, but what about Mrs. Thompson? She would be over seventy-five in, say, eighteen months and probably ready to retire.

"A possible pension arrangement was discussed," the minutes continue, "and ways and means of financing it were talked over and generous offers of help volunteered. [But if she preferred to stay on] we would be grateful if she felt like taking charge of the Children's Dept., for instance, as a part-time position for as long as she felt inclined if the trustees voted to engage another librarian to be in full charge as of Jan. 1954. We want to bring these matters up at a trustees' meeting but before doing so, we want to tell Mrs. Thompson of our plan and get her advice and co-operation. We therefore asked Miss Wardwell to talk over the situation with Mrs. Thompson that same evening."

Why Miss Wardwell in particular? Because she was known to be "most generous, thoughtful, and kind." Also, she had been the President of the Woodstock Club when it moved into the Lasher building so many years ago and when Alice Thompson became the "winter assistant." The two had been friends for a very long time.

Miss Wardwell willingly accepted the assignment; she thought she already knew how Alice Thompson felt about retiring since she herself had introduced the subject one day, some two years earlier, during lunch. "Of course I know I shall retire before a great while," she had said, "and I'm happy to say I can support myself for ten years. . . ." Miss Wardwell had not felt free to reveal to the Committee what had been said in confidence, but she remembered it as if it were yesterday.

Having arrived at what appeared to be a carefully thought-out plan for maintaining the library, it never occurred to any of those well-intentioned men and women that they had overlooked the very heart of the matter, namely, the emotional reaction of an elderly librarian who dearly loved her job when that dread specter Old Age (it already had a foot in the door) suddenly flung it wide open. Mrs. Thompson was unprepared, hurt, and indignant.

"Advise and co-operate indeed! Children's librarian? Never!"

Miss Wardwell, taken by surprise, was stunned and saddened.

The following Tuesday, with Mrs. Thompson grim-faced but firmly in charge, the library continued to function as usual.

29

Great Expectations Despite the Rain; Ugly Rumors; A Special Meeting

During June much had been accomplished. Under a new ruling library employees were now eligible for social security and both Mrs. Thompson and her assistant Margaret Brandon had signed the application papers. Rose Oxhandler had questioned Mr. Johnson, manager of Social Security Administration in Kingston, about Mrs. Thompson's status (over seventy-two) and her presumably pending retirement.

"Mr. Johnson assured me that Mrs. Thompson would receive monthly benefit checks of fifty dollars," Mrs. Oxhandler told the trustees during a board meeting on the 23rd, "if she continues to serve until January 1, 1954."

The trustees had listened with attentive interest to the secretary's report on the meeting at Miss Wardwell's and her account of her interview with Mrs. Thompson. And then, after some discussion, they were ready to vote.

"Mrs. Shirey moved that at the end of 18 months," the minutes read, "*barring unforeseen circumstances, Mrs. Wells will be offered the post of librarian. This was seconded by Mr. Neher and carried unanimously.*"

That summer the annual Fair, held on the last Thursday in July, did remarkably well despite the rain, which began at 3:00 and quickly eliminated the entire Midway display. It also slowed down sales at the tables but, thanks to the new attraction, "Great Expectations," the net returns remained high — $4236.19. The attention-catching name, proposed by the Fair Chairman, President "Dick" Richards, made a festive occasion of what was in fact a lottery, since a large number of tickets were sold of which only a few would win one or more of the many prizes donated by local merchants. But the people loved it and in the years to come the stakes would be well worth the gamble. For one dollar you might win a sports car or perhaps a U.S. Savings Bond.

At the library things appeared to be going as smoothly as ever. In September Mrs. Thompson entertained members of the Book Committee with a tea party in the garden of her home on DeLisio Lane. And that same month, at the board meeting, she surprised everyone by proposing that Mrs. Wells be appointed her assistant during the winter because both her daughter Betty, and her other assistant, Margaret Brandon, planned to be away for several months. Pleased by Mrs. Thompson's attitude, the trustees expressed their approval and Mrs. Wells, when asked if she would be willing to serve, readily agreed. A short time later, however, Mrs Schrader's plans changed. She would not be leaving Woodstock before January, she said, and would therefore continue to assist her mother until the first of the year. Would Mrs. Wells be available then? Again the answer was "yes."

The trustees had no reason to suspect that a storm was brewing until they learned that an ugly rumor was being spread through the village claiming that "some members of the board were seeking Mrs. Thompson's retirement for reasons of personal animosity." This was so false, so ridiculous, that they decided it was too silly to refute. They did, however, authorize the secretary to send Mrs. Thompson a report on the meeting at Miss Wardwell's "in the hope of clarifying a confused situation and to assure her that she was to retire only if and when financial security was made possible thru social security benefits and other means." *

* Presumably the Secretary had the discussion of "generous offers of help" in mind when she wrote "other means" — a vague term at best.

It was too late, however, to forestall what began as a trickle of letters questioning the board's action and gradually developed into a whirlpool of controversy. The first petition that arrived called for a special meeting of the members "so that the pros and cons of Mrs. Thompson's retirement could be talked over in a larger group."

A careful check of the membership list revealed that a third of the sixty-six of those who had signed the petition were not members of the library. Moreover, what were the "pros and cons" they planned to discuss? Mrs. Thompson's wish to stay on until she dropped in her tracks?

Because a large meeting could so easily deteriorate into a noisy exchange of conflicting views, the Executive Committee decided to invite the petitioners to send three of their number to meet with the board on December 18, at four o'clock. It was also decided that the offer by Jane Laws, one of the trustees, to record the meeting in shorthand should be accepted with thanks.

The invitation was accepted (with the sharp reminder that this was not what the petition had requested) and the three who arrived that Thursday afternoon were Henry Morton Robinson, the writer, Katrina Fischer, and Sidney Berkowitz, a retired businessman and former trustee.

With an eye to cutting the board down to size, Mr. Robinson expressed his "shock" at having learned that "Mrs. Thompson was now turned out to grass with no more quarter than a clerk."

Miss Wardwell was not easily intimidated. She spoke at length, explaining that "Mrs. Thompson had not suddenly been thrust out of the library . . . that she herself had been the first to speak of retiring . . . and when asked to take charge of the children's section, she had refused. A young man in the village says he will get his followers to fight this thing," Miss Wardwell added in a strained voice.

Intent on keeping the discussion as objective as possible,

Mr. Richards interposed: "I believe it would be useful to take a realistic look at the facts. First, Mrs. Thompson will be over seventy-five when she retires in another year. Second, the long hours of work and tension leave her exhausted by night. Third, the board feels it has faced up to its duty as tactfully as possible."

Mr. Robinson was willing to yield a little ground. He admitted that he thought the board had the right to retire its elderly librarian, but he did not see why, he said, "she should be expected to use her hard-earned savings to live on. Some formula should be worked out by which Mrs. Thompson would have some sort of augmented income. And unless we arrive at it here" — he paused to give emphasis to his words — "there are going to be *very unfortunate repercussions*. People may not be interested in coming to the Library Fair."

For Sidney Berkowitz, this came too close to brandishing a big stick. "Mrs. Thompson deserves more than money," he pointed out. "Certain recognition is due her as a retired person and she should be taken care of as well. Set up a pension fund — Miss Wardwell has made an offer of a very substantial gift [$1000] that might be the start of a campaign to raise a considerable amount of money. I would be willing to contribute not only money but my time to solve this problem."

"Mrs. Thompson is not alone in the world," Miss Wardwell said. "Her family is a very dignified and responsible family. She has a sister in Florida who would be glad to have her come and live there. I wish we could do something generous about her — she has been my friend."

"Should the trustees raise this money or should it be by public subscription?" Mr. Wetterau asked.

"The trustees should diligently explore the possibility of getting an increased annual amount from the village," Mr. Robinson insisted (as if all that was needed was a little diligence and the money would be forthcoming.) "This increased contribution could be earmarked as a pension for *all* librarians."

By this time Mr. Berkowitz was ready to offer a few concrete proposals of his own and when asked to frame a motion which Mrs. Leaycraft, as a trustee, could present to the board, he did so in the following words:

"That Mrs. Thompson becomes Librarian Emeritus on January 1, 1954 on half her present salary, and be made Honorary Life Member of the Library."

"This motion has been made, seconded and carried," President Richards said. "It is a recommendation to the board of trustees — now may I have a vote of confidence?"

"Not before we know what action the board will take," was Mr. Robinson's retort.

30

The Opposition Versus the Board

Houston Richards felt that he knew in advance how the board would react to the proposal that the librarian should be retired on half her present salary of $1400. How could the library carry the load? It would mean turning over to her the $600 received from the town and another $100 to boot. He also knew that there was not the ghost of a chance the town would increase its annual contribution to the library for any reason whatsoever. And he was correct on both counts.

The special meeting called to consider the proposed pension plan was held on Monday afternoon, December 29, and the motion was rejected as "financially unsound for the library" by a vote of 11 to 2. The two who had urged its acceptance were Mrs. Leaycraft and Kaj Klitgaard, a retired ship captain and ex-chairman of the Book Committee. After listening with mounting impatience to a discussion of other methods of raising funds (all of them impractical) Mr. Klitgaard warned that "in the case of Mrs. Thompson's retirement the so-called opposition is strongly organized."

"So it would seem," Mr. Richards said. "I have received another petition for a members' meeting and many letters to that effect, but I wholeheartedly agree with our secretary that it is both unnecessary and unfair to force a meeting in midwinter, when it is obviously impossible for the majority of the members to attend — also to deliberately stir up the town and promote public discussion of a matter that could be, and should be, settled in dignity and privacy between the trustees and the librarian. It is certainly bound to do more harm than good both to the library and to Mrs. Thompson. . . ."

"I went to see her this morning," Mrs. Summers said, "on my own initiative — without the approval or even the knowledge, of any other person whatsoever. . . . The statement she signed was a simple expression of her own sentiments, as expressed to me previously during chance meetings, at which, incidently, *she* introduced the subject. Let me read it to you: 'I deplore the ill-feeling which has been aroused by the continued public discussion of the plans for my retirement in January, 1954. In the interests of the Library I ask that no general members' meeting be called, because of this situation, before June, as I believe that before then the trustees and I will have resolved any remaining differences about the proposed arrangement.

Alice Putnam Thompson'

"I offered to leave it with her to consider and to return later in the day," Mrs. Summers continued, "but she said it was not necessary and would consult her advisers then and there. This she did by phone at some length — getting their consent and approval.

"The last thing she said to me as I was leaving was, 'You do whatever you like with it.' "

"Surely that is reason enough not to call a members' meeting before June," Mr. Wetterau said. "I saw Sidney the other day and he spoke of having talked with Alice Wardwell about the plan they have to launch an Alice P. Thompson retirement fund drive — but not until after the June meeting. So I move that Mrs. Thompson's statement be released to the press along with one by the board worded about like this: Because there has been a great deal of misunderstanding over the coming retirement of Mrs. Alice Thompson, the Board of Trustees of the Woodstock Library is making the following statement: That Mrs. Thompson will become Librarian Emeritus on January 1, 1954 and be made an honorary life member of the Library. That a substantial retirement gift will be made to her at that time. And it is suggested that friends of Mrs. Thompson raise a separate fund to which individual members of the board will be happy to contribute."

The entry in the minutes reads: "After further discussion this motion was passed [11 to 2] . . . to be released to the press immediately."

That same Monday, quite as if there was not a minute to spare — as if Mrs. Thompson was to be retired in another week rather than another year — the board's two dissenting members called a meeting of their group for that evening to discuss what could still be done "to make the board recognize its duty."

The outcome? Another petition insisting that a special meeting of all library members be called within two weeks "at which time a candid discussion of the whole matter of Mrs. Thompson's dismissal . . . shall proceed with or without them [the trustees]."

In his reply to this petition, dated December 30, 1952, President Richards leaned over backward in an attempt to pour oil on troubled waters by explaining in a friendly fashion that since so many members of the library were not in Woodstock at the time, it was "the considered opinion of the majority of the Board that such a meeting must be postponed until the annual Meeting at which time all the matters can be taken up after due consideration. . . ."

His letter, however, only served to add fuel to the flames. The same group sent another petition demanding that a members' meeting be called *"within two weeks."*

With the assistance of John Egan, a lawyer who had volunteered his services, Mr. Richard's letter in response to this latest petition was formal. He called attention to Article III, sections 7 and 8, which confer full power upon the trustees with respect to the employment of the librarian and to fix the retirement age of the librarian. "Under existing by-laws, therefore, the members cannot take any 'counter action' with respect to either of the matters referred to in the petition." It was a fairly long letter and the infuriated petitioners denounced it as being "shrouded in legal verbiage."

Scores of letters "To the Editor" were now appearing in the press, many of them signed by members of the "opposition." But the prize for absurdity goes to *The Wasp* of January 24, 1953. A short excerpt gives the flavor of the whole write-up headed "The Library Scandal." We quote: "Did you know that she [Mrs. Thompson] has been rudely, abusively and even sadistically used by the Board?"

This open rupture, this war of words waged in her behalf was almost more than Mrs. Thompson could take. She was extremely nervous and unhappy. It is possible, too, that she may have dreaded "breaking in" Mrs. Wells who, according to plan (her own, to be sure) would serve as her assistant during January and February, while Mrs. Thompson's daughter was away. So it may have been a relief to find that Mrs. Wells did not need constant coaching — in fact she was "quick to catch on" and Mrs. Thompson said as much. "You really know your alphabet," she told her. "I've found that few people actually do."

Although fragile in appearance, Mrs. Thompson, as Lynn Wells learned, did not lack backbone. She had a retentive memory for names and when she chanced to meet anyone on the street who had a book long overdue, he or she was requested in no uncertain terms to return it "right away."

Mrs. Thompson also had a puckish sense of humor. "While I was in the city," she recounted, "I tried to get one of our expensive art books from a young man who had borrowed it in the summer but hadn't returned it before he left in the fall. I knew where he lived and I was sure I could shame him into giving it to me when I asked for it. But when I knocked on his door and he opened it and recognized me he slammed it in my face. Of course that proved he did have the book. We never did get it back. I never saw him again. But it was rather an amusing adventure."

Mrs. Wells enjoyed library work. Even so, after Mrs.

Schrader's return she gladly set sail for a long vacation in Europe.

Early in May Betty Schrader informed the board that her mother was too ill to continue as librarian, whereupon the Executive Committee granted her an indefinite sick leave on full salary and appointed her two assistants, Mrs. Schrader and Mrs. Barbara Gibson (nee Herrick) who had replaced Mrs. Brandon, to serve "as long as necessary."

On May 25, the Executive Committee and an "advisory group of trustees" met to consider the status of those who would be entitled to vote at the annual meeting, scheduled for June 11. This year, in order to seat the large number expected to attend, the meeting would be held in the Town Hall. And the problem to be solved in advance was how to restrict the voting to members who had contributed a dollar or more to the library between May 1952 and June 1953, the day the notices would be mailed to the members. No new members, it was decided, would be accepted between June 5 and June 12. In other words, not until the day after the meeting. Even so, since "some members are away from Woodstock for long periods, but who have long supported the Library . . . by sending larger contributions but less often, with the understanding that it supports their voting status," they too would be eligible to vote.

News that those who had never taken out a membership or had allowed theirs to lapse would not be permitted to cast a vote quickly spread through the village, with the result that quite a large number of unexpected contributions of one dollar were received before the deadline of June 5. The dissenters were leaving no stone unturned. In her report, dated June 11, the chairman of the Membership Committee, Anita Smith, wrote: "One hundred and fifty-two additional members have paid their dues since May of 1952. Total membership entitled to vote at the annual meeting is 645, according to the rules of the Executive Committee."

The trustees were hopeful but far from certain as to how and where the chips would fall.

31

A Stormy Session; A Letter from Four Custodians

Since it seemed wise to have a complete record of the annual membership meeting to be held in the Town Hall on June 11, the Executive Committee engaged a court stenotypist. And all during the evening, despite the confusion, the interruptions and arguments, and, at times, shouted invectives, she appeared unperturbed, giving her full attention to her small machine.

A record high attendance jammed the hall, for this was the long-awaited showdown between the board of trustees and groups antagonistic to the retirement of Mrs. Thompson. The sense of tension was heightened by a printed statement distributed throughout the hall. It was a long detailed account, written by Mrs. Leaycraft, admonishing the board for its past actions, and urging the members to vote against "future lawlessness" by the trustees. And no sooner had the meeting got underway than the forces lined up against the board seized the opportunity to level a barrage of public criticism against the library's proposed plan to set aside $1500 as a pension fund, to be paid at the rate of $300 for five years. They questioned the library's budget, its bylaws, and finally the board itself, charging that it had been illegally elected [*] and was therefore subject to disintegration.

In short, throw out the charter and with it the board.

Supporters of the board answered with a counter battery which showed, when the smoke cleared away, that the

[*] A false charge — just one of many shouted from the floor.

132

trustees had acted under State laws and according to the commitments of the State Library charter. But the real triumph for the library came with the result of the voting (by ballot) for the board's slate of the six trustees whose four-year terms had expired, and three names to fill vacancies on the board. First, the board's slate followed by the number of votes cast:

Mr. George Compton	218
Mr. Alf Evers	214
Mrs. Hans Cohn	210
Mrs. William Shirey	199
Mrs. Dudley Summers	197
Mr. William Stifler	176
Mr. Lewis Wilson	173
Mrs. George Laws	173
Mrs. Elizabeth Baker	173

Then the ten names nominated from the floor:

Mr. Sidney Berkowitz	103
Mrs. Gertrude Robinson	97
Mr. Kaj Klitgaard	93
Mr. C. J. van Rijn	88
Mrs. Betty Crane	82
Miss Florence Hubbard	77
Mr. Richard Sharp	62
Mrs. Alice Johnson	46
Miss Alice Fischer	39
Mrs. Jean Mele	30

It was an overwhelming victory for the board's slate.

As the somewhat subdued crowd began to file out of the hall, one of the trustees, who happened to be standing near President Richards, saw a lady member of the opposition stalk up to him and spit in his face.

Shortly after the meeting in the Town Hall, the four who were directly concerned with launching a retirement fund campaign, as first proposed by Sidney Berkowitz at the petitioners' meeting with the board on December 18, 1952 and then incorporated in the library's published statement on December 29, met to compose a letter aimed to reach the hearts of all who had ever used a borrower's card.

Although the printed letter lacks a date, we know that it was mailed out well before the end of June.

The letter:

The Alice P. Thompson Retirement Fund

Woodstock, New York

CUSTODIANS

| Miss Alice Wardwell | Mr. Kaj Klitgaard |
| Mr. Sidney Berkowitz | Mr. John Pike |

Dear Woodstocker:

If you have ever been a member of the Woodstock Library, or used a borrower's card, or simply wandered in on a summer afternoon and browsed through the magazines, you may be interested in our plans.

Mrs. Alice Thompson has been our librarian for 26 years. It seems unlikely that anyone else in the community has come into contact with, and served, more individuals during this time than she. In fact, it might be said that what all of us — regardless of our age, income, or winter address — have most in common today in our friendship with Mrs. Thompson. She has known us; remembered our names; made our reading convenience her life's work.

Now that she is retiring, the Library Trustees are providing her with as large a pension as Library funds permit. This will amount to three hundred dollars a year for five years. The retirement fund which we are here proposing will not only supplement this provision, but will give each of us who have known Mrs. Thompson a personal, private opportunity to express our thanks to her.

Any of the above custodians will be happy to receive your contribution, in cash or by check, between now and her retirement. Further announcements, as to just when and how the fund will be presented to Mrs. Thompson, will appear in the local papers during the next few weeks.

Thank you for your consideration.

Yours sincerely,

Signed: ALICE W. WARDWELL
JOHN PIKE
KAJ KLITGAARD
SIDNEY BERKOWITZ

The *Catskill Mountain Star* ran a fairly long write-up about the fund under a two-column heading. It began by naming the "four prominent Woodstockers who have announced the establishment of an independent fund . . . in an effort to restore town harmony and provide additional funds for the retiring librarian," and then pointed out that they represented "both sides of the bitter controversy that has divided the village in recent months."

Doubtless contributions continued to trickle in for several weeks from those who had used the library or had taken an active interest in the whole unhappy affair, but as far as anyone knows there were no further announcements as to "when or how the fund would be presented to Mrs. Thompson."

Recently when John Pike, the only available member of the four who had signed the letter, was questioned about the amount raised during the drive, he confessed that he could remember nothing about the fund beyond having discussed the letter with Sidney Berkowitz at the time it was being written. As for the other three signers, two, we are sorry to report, had died (Mr. Berkowitz and Mr. Klitgaard) and Miss Wardwell, aged ninety in 1964, had left Woodstock to live elsewhere.

Even Mrs. Schrader had little to offer: "Whatever the amount was," she said, "it must have been deposited in Mother's savings account for her. I had nothing to do with it."

Like as not, by the end of the summer when Mrs. Thompson was consulted about "when and how" the contributions should be "presented" to her, she rejected the idea of being the subject of more publicity. She was no longer confined to her home, but she so dreaded further talk about her personal affairs that the plan to make a formal presentation was dropped and the money quietly banked for her.[8]

8. It may be worthwhile pointing out that the controversy over Mrs. Thompson's retirement took place during a period of national excitement which often approached hysteria. A committee headed by Senator Joseph R. McCarthy was making news with charges that communists had infiltrated high levels of American government; other Senate and House committees were charging that communists were prominent in the world of entertainment, education, and art and must be "rooted out." Many Americans were seeing conspiracies everywhere and in Woodstock, where so many people of varying beliefs and activities had come together since 1902, hostilities between the groups that made up the community were intensified or reshaped. The fact that Mrs. Thompson was not a Republican or Democrat but an active member of the Social Labor party and had upheld the library's policy of making available left wing as well as right wing books helped cause Woodstock people to choose sides in the controversy from the promptings of emotion rather than reason.

The library trustees had been unwilling to publicize such details as the lapses of memory against which Mrs. Thompson was so courageously struggling. This gave their actions a look of secrecy which some saw as evidence of a plot rather than evidence of a desire to spare their librarian's feelings. As both sides became locked into rigid positions, frank discussion of the problem became almost impossible. Elsewhere in the United States similar situations marked what is sometimes called the McCarthy era. [A.E.]

32

A Radio; The Fair; New Bylaws; A Hitch in Plans

As usual, the annual meeting of June 1953 was followed by a trustees' meeting during which the officers for the coming 12-month term were elected. It had been an unusually long members' meeting — two hours and forty minutes — and an extremely difficult one. Doubtless Houston Richards was more than glad to turn the gavel of his office over to his successor, Mrs. Herman (Rose) Oxhandler. She was succeeded as vice-president by Mrs. George (Jane) Laws.

Ahead lay a busy summer. The Fair scheduled for July 29 still lacked a chairman and at a special meeting held on June 18, the new president — a very up-and-coming person — solved that problem by dividing the responsibility into six parts with six chairmen in full charge of each section, such as food, clothing, books, and so on. She herself, she said, would serve as co-ordinator but only *when necessary*.

That settled, Mrs. Oxhandler felt free to pay a call on Mrs. Thompson. Still on sick leave, Mrs. Thompson was a lonely shut-in without even a radio to break the monotony. Here again was the sort of challenge Mrs. Oxhandler could take in stride. She asked the trustees to contribute money "out of their own pockets" for a radio.

"I've already been promised eighty-five dollars," she told the Executive Meeting on July 9, "and there's more to come. As soon as we know the final kitty we'll have Einer's Radio Service install the best possible radio for that price."

The entry in the minutes reads: "We all hope the radio will be a real comfort to her."

Now that the "well-organized opposition" had been revealed a paper tiger, its threatened boycott of the Fair was soon forgotten. Indeed, never before had there been a larger, better attended, more financially successful Library Fair. After all, this was the community's own library where you could get the books you wanted to read. Everyone was ready to bury the hatchet.

According to the minutes the gross intake was $7,865.64 with expenses listed as $620.27 plus one or two small outstanding bills, and credit was due to Lewis Wilson for his generous gesture of letting Great Expectations have for its first prize a car for exactly what it had cost him. The new secretary, Mrs. Elizabeth Baker (successor to Mrs. Summers) did not specify the make or kind of car. She called it "the magic car with its opulent net of $2,275." She also reported that Mrs. Oxhandler urged consideration of a "rough but permanent structure behind the Library to be used in winter as storage space for Fair equipment. . . ." It became a subject that cropped up repeatedly in the months ahead.

With the Library Fair over and done with, the Executive Committee concentrated on one of its most important problems — a careful revision of the bylaws. Mr. Egan had been consulted; the State Library had responded to a trustees' request that it send copies of approved bylaws used by other small libraries; and two members of the Committee had devoted many hours to drafting their own version of needed revisions.

It was Alf Evers who proposed that before the board voted to accept the final draft it should be read aloud at a special members' meeting to give everybody a chance to air his views. And so well did this suggestion work out that the opposing forces in the community moved several giant steps closer to harmony in the affairs of the library.

The meeting was not without its dramatic moments, but in spite of a few sarcastic remarks exchanged in the beginning, there was none of the turbulence and name-calling that marred the meeting in the Town Hall.

Most of the discussion revolved about a proposal from the floor that a clause be inserted in the bylaws authorizing five members to have a special meeting called by the president, provided the petition stated the matter to be discussed and was signed by fifty members. Mrs. Oxhandler assured the members that this recommendation would be given careful consideration by the board at the meeting which would follow the members' meeting. She then asked if there were any questions from the floor.

"I have one," Frank Mele said, rising. "How are the books for the library chosen — by the librarian?"

"I am a member of the Book Committee," Mr. Evers replied, "so let me say, yes, by the librarian with the help of the Book Committee; and that suggestions made from time to time by the readers are also considered."

This was followed by another question from a member who wanted to know how they decided when a book should be discarded from the shelves. And Mrs. Oxhandler herself supplied the answer. "If it has not circulated in five years or more and is not an especially valuable book, the librarian may discard it."

"The meeting adjourned very pleasantly," the secretary wrote, "and with much good feeling." She also noted later when recording the minutes of the board meeting that the motion to include the proposal made at the members' meeting for a special meeting to be called if signed by fifty members was "carried unanimously." As he left the meeting Mr. Stifler was heard to say that he hoped "the new bylaws would cover conditions not only for this year but for the next ten years."

Unfortunately the bylaws, for one reason or another, would be revised a number of times during the next decade. But never would there be any reference to a pension plan fund — the library was having difficulty enough in just keeping its financial chin above water. One clause would remain the same, however, for many years, namely the one concerning the librarian. It read: "A contract with the librarian may be renewed annually. The retirement age of the librarian shall be seventy years [in 1972, changed to sixty-five], except under special circumstances, when the age limit may be extended by the Trustees for a stated length of time."

The fact that Mrs. Thompson's sick leave had continued on throughout the summer [without any attempt on her part to resume her post] led to what the minutes called an "unexpected hurdle on Oct. 1." When Mrs. Thompson, accompanied by former President Klein, had gone to the Kingston office to apply for Social Security payments, "according to plan," the man in charge had declared that it made no difference whether or not she acted in an advisory capacity during her sick leave, or that she was being paid her full salary to the end of the year. In order to be eligible for Social Security payments, he said, Mrs. Thompson *must* return to work again and be seen in the library, both by townspeople and by inspectors from Albany.

But what about Mrs. Thompson's health? The board asked Betty Schrader if she felt that it would be safe for her mother to undertake part-time and curtailed work. "Yes," Mrs. Schrader replied, "if she is at the library only a few hours each week."

So for the time being things went smoothly enough, with Mrs. Thompson at the desk a few hours a week, to be seen by townspeople; and when another application for Social Security was made, it was accepted without question. But trouble lay ahead. When the first notification of her monthly payments was received it was learned that instead of the $50 counted upon, she would be getting only $26 monthly until April 1954, at which time the amount would be raised "to $30, approximately, on a retroactive basis."

Greatly puzzled and concerned, a search was made through library records of the previous year and from these Mrs. Laws found that it was Mr. Johnson of the Kingston office who had told the trustees "during a conversation" that the monthly Social Security payments would be $50. It now appeared that he had been mistaken and although the library was under no legal obligation to make good the difference, the trustees willingly voted a monthly contribution of $25 from the library to be paid for "one year out of the 1954 budget and reconsidered annually when preparing each succeeding year's budget."

In short, the board would make sure that Mrs. Thompson's annual income would be $900 for the next five years.

33

The New Staff; A Merry-go-round; A Carillon

In the summer of 1953 when Lynn Wells returned from her vacation in Europe she learned for the first time that Mrs. Thompson had had a nervous breakdown and that there had been a history-making fracas in the Town Hall. Betty Schrader had been substituting for her mother at the library, Mrs. Wells was told, but the Executive Committee would greatly appreciate it if she would begin in November rather than two months later, as originally planned.

So it was that Lynn Wells became librarian on Tuesday, November 3, with one assistant, Kay (Mrs. Orestes) Cleveland. The two made an excellent team: both were warm, friendly women who enjoyed the work. They willingly accepted the Executive Committee's proposal that the library be open one night a week — preferably a Friday night, and at a subsequent meeting Mrs. Wells reported that attendance on Friday evenings, since the inauguration "of this new service has been successively four, six, eleven, four, two." Evidently there was no crying need for the library to be open evenings; even so, the experiment was continued and after a while attendance did increase.

In a letter addressed to her "Fellow Trustees," dated November 19, 1953, Rose Oxhandler, who was wintering in Florida, said: "I would like your approval for an expenditure in connection with a merry-go-round that was donated to us by a friend of Lewis Wilson. They are building a platform and fixing the machinery as their contribution. We need the horses and we have found someone who can make them, who is willing to carve and finish 6 wooden horses for us for $200. Please vote yes for this project."

The "someone" who could make the horses proved to be William Spanhake, the owner of the sawmill in Wittenberg. He was an old hand at carving wooden animals, having learned the art as a young man in Hanover, Germany, and he was known to be still at it, working on and off in his spare time. Before leaving Woodstock, Mrs. Oxhandler had gone to Mr. Spanhake's house to ask if he would carve six horses for the Fair's merry-go-round.

"The library couldn't pay more than two hundred dollars," she said to him. "I know that isn't much but you'd have all winter; we wouldn't want them before April or May."

Mr. Spanhake had needed a little time in which to think it over so he offered to show Mrs. Oxhandler his workshop. "It's up on the second floor," he said. The room was not large, the workbenches took up much of the space and there was a lingering smell of carpenter's glue and wood shavings. After pointing out some of the things he had been carving, he went on to explain how all fine merry-go-round horses are made. "They're always hollow," he said, "otherwise they'd be too heavy. And they're carved in sections with each piece complete down to the last detail; the ears, eyes, teeth, mane and tail. Even the bridle and saddle are made of wood. And before the parts are glued together the inner side is treated with hot linseed oil — that's to preserve the wood. I prefer basswood or poplar — native wood grown right here — and I always make my own designs."

Mrs. Oxhandler was not easily sidetracked: she was a persistent person. Mr. Spanhake finally agreed to carve the horses "because it's for the library."

Although the committee in charge of assembling the merry-go-round must have realized that insurance to cover its operation during the afternoon of the Fair would have to be carried by the library, no one seems to have inquired what the cost would be until after the horses had been finished but for a final coat of paint. In April the committee was in for a big surprise: the figure quoted by the insurance company was so unbelievably high that it was declared "prohibitive" and the project was cancelled on the spot. Mr. Spanhake had kept his end of the bargain, but what could be done with the horses?

We turn to the minutes of the April meeting for the answer. Anita Smith, who was serving as secretary *pro tem,* wrote: "The Executive Comm. recommended buying the six horses ordered from Mr. Spanhake last fall. These wooden horses may be sold at auction for more than the $200 now being paid for them. Miss Smith suggested asking well-known artists to decorate them for this purpose. A list of artists was submitted."

She, herself, being chairman of the Book Committee, could think of two names: "We might ask Arnold Blanch and Doris Lee to do one of the horses — they're both members of my committee now."

"Miska Petersham is a trustee, he and his wife Maud would do a wonderful job, they're such fine artists," someone proposed. And so the list grew: Edward Chavez, Julio deDiego, Howard Mandel, and one or two others.

Here was a unique solution to a difficult problem — even the artists who were asked to decorate the horses were enthusiastic.

In May the library received a copy of a letter sent from Woodstock, England, to the Secretary of the Historical Society of Woodstock, New York.

Dear Sir:

I am writing to inform you of a project to arrange this summer an exhibition "Woodstocks of the World" in the Town Hall of

Woodstock, England, in the hope that your town might be interested and would wish to be associated with the exhibition. . . . There has been a carillon in Woodstock Church since the 18th century and it continued to play a different tune each day of the week until the war, when all church bells were silenced to be ready as a warning of enemy invasion. After the war it was found that age and disuse had taken their toll and it was decided to commemorate the sesquicentennial by restoring the carillon and installing an electrically driven mechanism to play the same tunes that had been heard over 200 years. It then occurred to some of us that other Woodstocks in the world — there are probably about 40: 9 in Australia, 3 in Canada, 3 in New Zealand, 1 in South Africa and about 23 in the United States — might wish to be associated with a communal memorial cementing these bonds of friendship which community of language and fundamental ideals maintain. . . . The response to this proposal was most heartening; our first reply came from Woodstock, Connecticut, the oldest after our own town, then we heard from Woodstock, Ontario, the largest of all the Woodstocks, and now we have received donations and support from many other Woodstocks in the North American Continent and Australasia. However, we are anxious that on the plaque commemorating this world-wide community of spirit will be inscribed the names of all Woodstocks that wish to join in our enterprise and that is one of the reasons that I am writing to you. The other reason is, that even if you have no desire to join with us, you would be willing to send me information and illustrations about your Woodstock, its history and famous citizens, its present activities, appearance, resources and so forth for the exhibition. We have many visitors to Woodstock each summer from all over the world, as it is a short distance from the ancient University town of Oxford, and is on the route to Stratford-on-Avon, while Blenheim Palace, the home of the Dukes of Marlborough, and the birthplace of our Prime Minister, Sir Winston Churchill, is situated at Woodstock. . . . Our Woodstock is a small market town with about 2000 inhabitants, the center of a mixed farming community and having as its principal industry glovemaking, which has been carried on here since the days of Queen Elizabeth I; if you would be interested I could send you a small illustrated booklet giving the account of our town.

> Hoping to hear from you,
> With all good wishes to you all,
> Yours faithfully,
> A. H. T. Robb-Smith, M.D.
> Chairman,
> Woodstock Chimes Committee

The trustees listened attentively while Mrs. Oxhandler, who had returned in April, read the letter, then voted to contribute $10 to the fund and to send "appropriate historical and pictorial materials for the British group." A rather small sum, it would seem, in light of the library's cornerstone from Blenheim Palace. The small illustrated booklet mentioned in the letter arrived in due time and is still among the library's papers. The following month $50 was collected from "various sources" in the community and sent to the Chimes Committee in England.

34

A Map; An Auction and a Name for the Horse

It was with "deep regret" and only because she was far from well that Rose Oxhandler resigned as president in June of 1954. Vice-President Laws after some hesitation agreed to succeed Mrs. Oxhandler for one term. The fact that Jane Laws would remain in office for three consecutive years (thus setting a record) and prove to be one of the best, most active presidents in many years is a matter of record.

Jane Laws had a reputation for devoting herself whole-heartedly to whatever she undertook, and for the new president the Fair, scheduled for Thursday July 29, would be a real challenge even though experienced chairmen were already deep in plans for handling the many details. By this time the annual Fairs had become so large and so diversified that it took endless planning to find space for the midway, the flea market, the games, books, the eight or nine racks for and clothing in addition to all the many, many other tables and booths.

"I'm sure we could save time and avoid much of the confusion," Mrs. Laws told the chairman of the Fair Committee, Gertrude Robinson, "if we had a map to follow, a map showing the location of every single department in relation to the trees, the library and the brook. And I believe my husband would be willing to make just such a map."

The brook? Today only the old-timers remember the shallow brook, rich with masses of watercress and spanned by a narrow footbridge, for it has long since gone underground. But from the first it had been the bane of the Fair because so many inattentive visitors stumbled into the brook to emerge wet to the ankles and mad as hornets. Fed by a spring on Victor Lasher's place, it flowed eastward across his large field in front of the library and then, via a culvert under the road, into Tannery Brook.

An engineer by training, George Laws knew exactly what was needed: he drew the map to scale — one inch to ten feet — with every department labeled: china, balloons, crazy hats, hot dogs, and so on. There was even a place for the platform on which the Great Expectations car would be on exhibition. He did not have to take the horse auction into account, however, because the owners of the laundromat across the road had granted permission to hold it in front of their building.

The plan to have the hand-carved horses decorated by local artists had worked out remarkably well and the press, upon receiving the advance publicity, had played it up for all it was worth. The *Kingston Daily Freeman* sent a reporter to interview Mr. Spanhake and snap a picture of him at work in his shop, chisel and mallet in hand. The *Woodstock Press* ran a story under a two-column headline: "Library Fair Opens Thurs. Features Horse Auction," and went on:

> One of Woodstock's oldest traditions — the Library Fair — which opens next Thursday at noon, will have a new twist this year — a merry-go-round horse auction. Woodstock's auctioneer LaMonte Simkins is ready to sell to the highest bidder five beautifully carved and painted steeds. . . .

An uninformed reader might find this a bit misleading since it seemed to imply that all five steeds would go to the highest bidder. Actually, they would be auctioned off one by one. But why only *five* horses when the minutes twice speak of six? The answer to that question was never recorded.

Auctions of almost any kind had long been popular in town and when LaMonte Simpkins was the auctioneer he kept things going at a lively pace. In fact, it was not unusual for him to lead some inexperienced bidder to raise his own bid — much to the amusement of everyone else. So on the afternoon of the Fair, at three o'clock to be exact, when the voice of the master of ceremonies, Houston Richards, came blaring over the loudspeaker, the word "auction" caught the attention.

"Ladies and gentlemen," he shouted, "members of the Woodstock Riding Club are in charge of the corral across the road. They will handle the five prancing merry-go-round horses about to be sold at auction. Go now and bid against the other fellow. Become the proud owner of a unique example of an all-but-lost art, a hand-carved, hand-decorated horse, painted and signed by some of Woodstock's most famous artists. Here's the chance of a lifetime. Hurry, hurry, hurry. . . ."

In the beginning, despite the auctioneer's best efforts, the bidding lagged. The horse decorated by Arnold Blanch brought only $50, but after that things began to pick up. Julio deDiego's bright aqua horse went to Mrs. Charles Cooper for $100; Dr. and Mrs. Norbert Beim, guests at Pinecrest Lodge, gave $105 for the Howard Mandel decorated horse; and the one painted by Edward Chavez went for $100 to the Weathervane Shop, across from the fire house.

The chairman of Great Expectations' Car Committee had been waiting to bid on the horse so beautifully decorated by Maud and Miska Petersham, whose books for children were widely known and well loved. The Committee planned to give it to the library for the children's room and when no one topped her final bid — $100 — the prancing steed with its golden mane and tail was assured of a permanent home and the admiration of countless youngsters.

Shortly after the Fair a story appeared in the *Woodstock Press*. The new horse had no name, it seemed, therefore all children of ten years of age or younger were invited to come to the library, to see the horse and write the name of their choice on a slip of paper. "In about two weeks all the names will be looked over by Mrs. Lynn Wells and Mrs. Orestes Cleveland, librarians, and the best 10 will be set aside. Then the children will be invited to come to a story hour and the youngest child present will draw one slip from the bag of ten names. The name drawn will be the name of the horse."

Appropriately enough, the name on that slip of paper was Peter — short for Petersham.

35

A Storage Problem

Never before in the twenty-three-year history of Library Fairs had there been one so successful as the Fair of 1954 — topping the record-breaking net of the previous year. Again we quote the *Woodstock Press:*

A total of $9,000 was grossed at the Library Fair which lasted just five hours last Thursday on the Library Grounds. Although figures are still not complete, a net of $8200 was expected. The 1954 Ford, which alone netted $3200, was awarded to Mrs. Eugene Speicher, at the close of the Fair, amid disappointed groans from expectant onlookers.

Library Fair treasurer Albert Wangler cautioned, however, that any figures announced at this time were still approximate. The final figures won't be complete, he said, until after the Board of Trustees meeting August 12 . . . thousands of persons, many of them from out of town, thronged the Library Fair grounds despite the heat of the day. Thunderstorms early in the morning gave way to sunshine for the fair from noon to five, and then obligingly started again at 6 P.M. dampening only the cleanup committee who struggled with the heroic mounds of watermelon rinds and orange drink containers.

During the sunlit hours, all was gaiety. The puppet show put on by Mrs. Margaret Wetterau's Guild workshop was charming and original and drew a fascinated crowd of youngsters. Brightly colored zinnias and other flowers made a Parisian scene of the flower booth, and Max Angiell inflated a steady stream of balloons, many of which floated skyward, while small owners watched regretfully until the brightly-colored globes disappeared. Fun hats, made by Mrs. Jay Alan [Allen] were seen throughout the crowd and Mrs. Alexander Semmler predicted many a fortune with cards. Hundreds of souvenirs of Woodstock faces peering through cut-out cardboard figures of spacemen and circus characters were sold by Mrs. John Striebel who had taken them with her Polaroid camera.

Another highpoint of the Fair was LaMonte Simpkin's auction of wooden horses. . . .

Great Expectations sold $645 worth of tickets, $31 more than last year. . . .

Always punctilious about details, Mrs. Laws saw to it that a full record concerning the Fair was typed out and carefully preserved: "Mr. Albert Wangler read the Financial Report [Final Business Meeting, August 9] which was not complete: Gross Proceeds $8,991.49; Expenses to date: $823.84; bal. $8,167.65. Approximated Exp. $200; Approximated net $7,990.65." There were pages and pages filled with the names of everyone who had worked on the afternoon of the Fair: the table chairmen, their co-chairmen and assistants, along with their reports, conclusions and suggestions for future fairs. Most impressive of all was the way the Grounds Chairman, William Stifler, had listed by name every single piece of fair equipment owned by the library and where each item was stored for the winter: the McTiege barn, the library's tool shed and "attic" — the small space under the sloping roof on the second floor.

Before 1952 one of the most difficult problems had been finding a more or less centrally located place to be used as a collection center where people could leave articles they were donating to the coming Fair. For example, in late June of 1951 a notice appeared in the papers informing the public that articles for the Library Fair "will be gratefully accepted at any time at the home of Houston Richards in Byrdcliffe." It would seem that the chairman of that fair was shouldering more than his share of the work.

The following year and again in 1953 the library gladly gave the Methodist Church $25 for the use of its Hall as a collection center prior to the Fair and another $10 to the person who cleaned up the place afterwards. And every time the proposal to build a permanent storage and collection center had been discussed at a board meeting it had been either voted down or tabled. One trustee had said she thought that library money should be spent for books rather than for a shed; another felt that a shed out back would hurt the appearance of the property. Mr. Stifler thought that the proposed building "wasn't actually needed."

Acting on a motion made by David Carlson at the August meeting, Mrs. Laws appointed a committee of five to make a detailed analysis of the matter and report back at the September meeting. The five, William Stifler, Chairman, Hilde Cohn, Isabel Doughty, George Neher, and Alf Evers took their assignment as a survey committee seriously. In their ten-page report they tried, they said, to evaluate the library's *needs* rather than the means of satisfying these needs. Many who had been active in past Fairs were questioned, so was each member of the Book Committee. The library's stock of books had doubled during the past twenty years, it was learned, but "the rate of discard of obsolete or seldom used books has recently been stepped up [Mrs. Wells and her assistant had been spending an hour a day weeding out during their inventory of the fiction] and television is reported to be slowing down the rate of library book-borrowing elsewhere and may have similar effects here. . . . Actual counts of various types of books in the Library show our present stocks of art, music, and other books, to be as follows: Art 1300, Music 600, Reference 160, Poetry 525, Drama 450. . . Together, all these groups take up, on the shelves, about one quarter of the wall shelves in the new wing. . . ."

This committee turned in a long report explaining why it had concluded that "for the present, no additional space or building are actually necessary."

Appointed at the same time to investigate the *cost* of the proposed Fair Building (no longer called a storage shed) was a second committee of five: Lewis Wilson, Chairman;

David Carlson; Thomas Dendy; Herbert Wyman; and John Pike. Their report stated that "any suggestion that the Fair is outmoded", that the new building was not needed "would be entirely without basis. . . ." Dire things could happen to the library, the report warned, if, by failing to remain largely self-supporting, it was taken over by the town and was under the management and control of the Town Board rather than "this Board." Possibly they did not realize that a chartered public library, whether under the "control" of the Town Board or a group of private citizens, serving as trustees, is subject to New York State Library laws. Even so, the second Committee still had trump cards to play. It presented a watercolor sketch by John Pike of the proposed building; a map drawn to scale showing the exact relation of the new structure to the tool shed, the library and the boundary lines of the property. The estimate submitted by Karl Schroeder, a local contractor, figured the cost for a 52′ x 24′ building, including the wiring, gutterwork and two coats of exterior paint at $3,860. "That represents about three dollars a square foot," Lewis Wilson said, "and I consider it extremely low."

When the two reports were discussed at the September meeting and the treasurer gave the funds on hand as a total of $16,771.92, many of the trustees who had previously opposed the project appeared to change their mind, but it may have been what Miss Wardwell said that turned the tide. "The most valuable and precious commodity we have is the cooperative friendship of the town of Woodstock. Realizing the exhausting and heroic efforts the Library's friends have made, we should give them every consideration in making their task lighter. The Fair building would be a concrete evidence of our appreciation. If we can afford it, we should go ahead fearlessly."

"Miss Wardwell's statement was greeted with applause," the secretary wrote.

The vote, by ballot, was eighteen in favor of the erection of the building, three against.

36

Volunteers; A Brochure; Memorial Funds

Now that the question of the Fair Building had been settled (the contractor promised to have it completed by May 1, 1955), the trustees were free to devote themselves to the more run-of-the-mill needs of the library. The secretary, Noelle N. Gillmor, was directed to acknowledge "with warmest thanks" the contribution of $150 from the Woodstock School Board.

It was a welcome gift since the town was still unwilling to increase its annual donation of $600. Nevertheless, apart from having to keep an eagle eye on proposed expenditures (the purchase of sixty suitable folding chairs provided the cost did not exceed $300), everything was going extremely well. In December the chairman of the Membership Committee, Hilde Cohn, reported that in 1953 there had been a marked increase in the number of book borrowers who had paid annual dues — 390 had contributed $1103. But what no one seemed to have pointed out was this: the marked increase in membership was due in large part to those who had hustled to hand in a dollar just before the June meeting in order to vote against the Board.

The staff, Lynn Wells and Kay Cleveland, with over a year's experience behind them, were handling the work with ease; and when Mrs. Wells's contract was renewed it was "with an expression of deep appreciation for the superb work she is doing." But no mention was made in the minutes of the many volunteers who did the workaday jobs that were an intrinsic part of keeping the library on its feet.

For example, there was the Mending Committee. It met

once a week at the library to repair books with weak spines, dog-eared corners, and loose leaves, thus saving the cost of replacement — especially for the books perused by youngsters. Then there was the volunteer who took reading matter to the elderly. This involved far more than merely transporting books from the library to the person's home because the volunteer had to keep track of when the books were due, call for them — and sometimes help search for missing ones among piles of old newspapers, magazines, and paperbacks. Furthermore, there was the tricky problem of selecting the right sort of book (with the help of the staff) for each individual shut-in.

The volunteers (not always the same ones by any means) who met each spring prior to mailing out the membership letters had a tiresome job because of the amount of work involved. Those capable of addressing envelopes in a clear hand were seated at the long table in the wing where they plied their pens. Close by, at the large round table, was the group that folded each printed letter and tucked it, together with a return envelope, into the hand-addressed envelope, then sealed it. The next step took place not in the library but at the post office and this, too, was carried out by volunteers. The application by hand of many hundreds of stamps was a tedious job and the trustees knew it. A letter from Noelle Gillmor to Bea Ostrander, dated May 13, 1958, reads as follows:

Dear Bea,

As another Membership mailing goes out, we realize once again how much we owe to you in helping us do an efficient job in reaching our supporters. All of us at the Library want to tell you that we are deeply grateful to you and to your colleagues for getting this job out and for the innumerable other ways in which you have personally helped us in our work.

It's people like you that make working for the Library a pleasant — and so often a successful — venture.

So, again, thanks a million times.

The largest number of volunteers involved in a single project was, of course, composed of those who carried the heavy load of making the yearly Fair a success. But so much could be said about them that it would be beyond the scope of this book. This much, however, is crystal clear: without the volunteer workers there would have been no Woodstock Club's fledgling library; there would be no Woodstock Library as we know it today.

By mid-March the committee in charge of the spring membership drive was already up to its ears in plans for a brochure to be enclosed with its annual letter — a brochure telling about the various services provided by the library, how it functioned, and so on.

There was no question as to who, among the trustees, could best prepare such a booklet: Alf Evers, an established writer, was eminently fitted to write the sort of copy that would stir public interest and give Woodstockers a sense of pride in their library, and when he graciously accepted the assignment its success was assured.

"Is the Library a Luxury?" was his opening line.

Many a stranger wandering into the Woodstock Library on a hot, summer afternoon in search of no more than a place to sit down has been surprised by the Library's size, scope and efficiency. For our Library is not like the ones on which many other communities still limp along — the kind that are open only a few hours a week under the care of some worthy soul with all the good will in the world but no library training at all. In such libraries, book lovers may browse among the kind of books grandma read — Victorian novels, and guides to travelling in the 1880's plus a handful of the lightest of recent books. Luckily, our Library is different. It is true, however, that it gives shelfroom to many light books. . . . But a modern library like ours does more than this — far more. It supplies useful, practical information, help toward better citizenship and living, and the inspiration that comes of an acquaintance with the many aspects of human culture. Our Library is no luxury — the job it does is necessary if Woodstock is to remain a good place to live in. . . .

We are then told that the Woodstock Library operates on the assumption that "children are very important," and that it devotes a high percentage of its budget to children's books. Furthermore, when the storyteller entertains groups of children on Saturday mornings she "helps them to form the good habit of using their library." And that it is a good place too for the artists, musicians, writers, and other creative people of the community "because of the special collections in their fields — books on art alone numbering 1300." The library's need for financial support was neatly covered in one amusing paragraph called "Operation Bootstrap: Under the plan, each member would take a firm grip on his bootstraps and lift himself up one notch in the scale of membership." By this simple means "one dollar members would become two dollar members, five dollar members would become ten dollar members and ten dollar members would be heartily welcomed into the thin ranks of the twenty-five dollar members."

Then comes a brief mention of the library's early years, the devoted service of Librarian Emeritus Alice Thompson and the gift of the building by Mrs. Weyl in memory of her husband.

"This building links us to the Woodstock of the pioneer doctor Larry G. Hall which housed his cherished medical library of sixty volumes. Recently Woodstock people have established the custom of keeping fresh the memories of friends no longer with us by making gifts of funds for buying books or needed equipment. In this way the memories of Alice Henderson, Yasuo Kuniyoshi and Eugen Schleicher [of the Jack Horner Shop] have been honored. . . ."

What are still known as Memorial Funds originated in

August, 1954, with a gift of $100 from the "Blanch Group" in memory of the Japanese artist Yasuo Kuniyoshi, long a resident of Woodstock. The donation was to be used (it was specified) for the purchase of art books to be chosen by Arnold Blanch, Doris Lee, and Reginald Wilson. This was followed, four months later, by a second contribution. According to the minutes, "Miss Agnes Schleicher informed the librarian that friends of her late father had been asked to send contributions to the Library instead of flowers to the services, for the purchase of books about Ghandi and Albert Schweitzer."

In the treasurer's report for February 1955 there are two entries relating to the funds: "Kuniyoshi, balance $65.85; Schleicher, balance $62"; and from then on the amounts on hand dwindled to a close.

The gift in memory of Alice Henderson, an active member of Anita Smith's Extension Committee, took a different form. Early in 1954 a local carpenter had been commissioned to build the large, handsome librarian's desk that would replace the old inadequate one where books were checked out. This was the first piece of library equipment purchased with memorial money, and embedded in the top of the desk is a brass plaque bearing the following inscription:

> Presented To The
> Woodstock Library
> By the Friends of
> Alice Henderson
> 1954

More about the Memorial Funds presently, but before we leave the fourth and best in the library's series of brochures, a word about the reproduction of the photograph on its cover, a photograph taken during the winter by Konrad Cramer. It gives a panoramic view of the old building as seen from the parking lot, with the wooden stormshed on the front porch. Midway along the east side of the library is the small side porch and door that was used until the trustees decided "the front door was the proper entrance." And on beyond we get a glimpse of the end of the wing and the new Fair Building.

37

Eyewitness Reports; Offers Politely Refused

Clipped in with the May minutes of 1955 is a note addressed to the president and written by Jane Shirey for her ailing mother, Kay Cleveland. "I cannot tell you how *deeply* affected I am to learn that the Board has voted me a two-months' vacation with *my pay*. . . . It means so much to me for the thought and kindness behind it. You can imagine how eager I am to get back to the most pleasant job in the world!"

The letter bore no date but Mrs. Laws mentioned it during her report at the annual meeting in June which gives us a clue — of sorts. And we know that Georgia Lingafelt, a newly elected trustee, volunteered to fill in for Kay temporarily. The Book Committee had welcomed Miss Lingafelt with open arms and well it might. Before coming to Woodstock she had run such a special sort of bookshop in Chicago that she was known by her large clientele as the "Sylvia Beach" of that city — a compliment indeed considering the fame of Miss Beach's *Shakespeare and Company* in Paris.

In August, however, Mrs. Cleveland was granted an indefinite leave of absence because she had had to return to the hospital for further treatment and Ethel Moncure was engaged as substitute assistant.

Both names — Miss Lingafelt and Mrs. Moncure — will reappear again as our narrative progresses. There is one name in particular, however, that has continued to appear in the minutes many times for many years — that of Anita Smith. She was a volunteer who could be counted on to work with enthusiasm at the Fair year after year wherever help was most needed. Then she would do what few others were capable of, i.e., turn in entertaining eyewitness reports.

In 1954 she wrote: "People come from miles around know-ing they will find good entertainment for themselves, while their children delight in Magic Shows, sometimes a trained seal, a pony ride, or at least a carrousel. The artists' Gypsy orchestra roams through the grounds, while people rush to buy such items as a Paris gown for fifty cents, or a dining room table for a quarter from the Flea Market. The Town Supervisor cooks hot dogs, a symphony orchestra leader ped-dles balloons, a cartoonist snaps portraits, and actors parade in costume, while pretty girls sell bouquets of flowers. Ban-ners wave in the mountain breeze, tambourines jingle, young people shout with laughter and all the while with painless effort enough money pours into the cash boxes to support the Library for another year."

Another of Miss Smith's accounts (undated) tells about the Flea Market and how people haggled over the price of a picture frame and broken furniture without "suspecting that the quiet salesman might be a famous artist." One year George Bellows made drawings of individuals for a dollar and this set Miss Smith to wondering what would become of the portrait drawings — drawings that might be worth, even-tually, hundreds of dollars.

"The well-known orchestra director, Leon Barzin," she wrote, "had the job of blowing up hundreds of balloons for the children. Oh those kids, what a holiday it was for them! . . . they had puppets, magic or pet shows to enjoy, the 'pets' being anything from a caterpillar to a llama. . . . The best-loved performer was Sharkey the seal. It was through his appearance at the Fair that he secured a part in a Broadway show and went ahead to movie fame. He was a co-star in the show *Higher and Higher*. Children are frequently misplaced but never lost. The [retired] actor Houston Richards who for years has been Master of Ceremonies, with the job of an-nouncing these incidents through a loud-speaker, says 'it is the parents not the children who are lost.'

"Around the booths the crowds whoop, the hawkers shout

their wares, the sunshine flickers over the flowers and vegetables and the music makes everybody happy. Faster and
faster the money jingles into boxes and the Library budget
will be met for another year."

That summer Anita Smith, still chairman of the Book Committee, reported that the library had received an offer of
two hundred books on aviation, with the proviso that they
never be sold. In her reply to the would-be doner, Miss
Smith said, "Unfortunately we have to refuse all collections
that conflict with the Library's right eventually to discard
them if their space would be required for volumes in greater
demand. We thank you very much for your offer."

In September an offer of a very different sort was received.
The letter asked the board to consider building an addition
to the present structure which could be used to house,
permanently, at least some of the paintings by the late
Herminie Kleinert, to exhibit work of other artists in the
community, and "if possible to provide a place for informal
concerts and musical gatherings. Mrs. Lenore Marsh has
tentatively offered $25,000 for this purpose," the letter con-
cluded.

Certain of the trustees frankly stated that they considered
the sum mentioned as inadequate, especially in regard to
maintenance and upkeep.

"The capital for upkeep should at least equal the capital
for construction," Mrs. Rosett declared. "We must make certain such an addition would be truly an asset and not a lia-
bility."

The treasurer, Thomas Dendy, added: "And *not* a museum
for a private collection."

But it was Lewis Wilson who took the long view. "The
library's available building space is so limited," he said, "we
must be careful how it is used — actually only for purposes
directly beneficial to it."

In December, after lengthy consideration, the board by
unanimous vote politely refused the offer. And as time would
prove, it was a wise decision indeed.

38

The Lasher Field; The First Newsletter

During the early part of 1956 with everything going smoothly at the library, the minutes for the most part were reports on routine matters. In August, however, the board learned that Mrs. Thompson was ill. For the first two years after her retirement she had wintered in Florida, returning in the spring to her home in Woodstock. But now she was no longer able to travel, her daughter said, and must remain in Woodstock. Whereupon the trustees voted to release at once the sum remaining in the Thompson "trust fund" which amounted, with interest, to $683.

Much to everyone's pleasure, Kay Cleveland had returned to the library in mid-summer looking fit and very happy. But in less than two months she was again granted an indefinite sick leave and Ethel Moncure was again engaged as her replacement.

Meanwhile plans were under way for a step of vital importance to the library. A committee of three — Jane Laws, David Carlson, and Thomas Dendy — had been appointed to discuss with Victor Lasher the possibility of buying the large field out front where the annual Fairs had been held for the past twenty-five years. They were urged "to confer with him as promptly as possible."

In September Mrs. Laws was ready with her report. Mr. Lasher's first reaction, she told the Board, was that he had "no interest in selling the land." But just as the three were leaving he reversed himself. "Let's put it this way," he said, "I'll gladly listen to an offer."

"The next step," the minutes continue, "is to wait for a

figure from two appraisers in Kingston." Several of the trustees, however, did not like the idea of waiting: they wanted to strike while the iron was hot and proposed offering Mr. Lasher $3,000.

No time was lost in conveying the library's offer, but three months would elapse before his reply was recorded. In December, David Carlson told the board that Mr. Lasher was giving the offer "serious consideration" and advised "that no further steps be taken pending Mr. Lasher's decision."

By October it had become evident that Kay Cleveland was far too ill to return to her post as assistant librarian and when it was proposed that her salary be continued until January 1, 1957, the vote in favor was unanimous. There had been six applications, Mrs. Laws said, and Mrs. Charles Boswell had been appointed to replace Mrs. Cleveland.

The board's generous decision to keep Kay Cleveland's name on the payroll was much appreciated by her family since it served to bolster her hope that she might indeed recover. Unfortunately, Mrs. Cleveland did not live to see the new year. In December, soon after her death, her family requested that "her salary be kept by the Library" as part of a memorial fund to which a further contribution of $200 would be made — the money "to be used in any way the Library saw fit."

With the Kay Cleveland Fund which, as of February 1957, amounted to $330, the Book Committee welcomed the opportunity to purchase a much-needed new edition of the *Encyclopaedia Britannica*. And since Mrs. Cleveland's family had stated that the library could use the contributions in any way it saw fit, the board also voted to purchase a drinking fountain.

But why, of all things, a drinking fountain at the Woodstock Library? Because the two librarians were finding the many requests by thirsty youngsters for a glass of water, please, troublesome. Each time one or the other of them had to stop what she was doing and go into the small kitchen off the office to fetch a glass of water. Even so, due to technical difficulties, the installation of the drinking fountain would be delayed many months.

For the Woodstock Library, March 4 should have been a red-letter day: exactly thirty years earlier a reception had been held to celebrate the opening of the Club's library in its new quarters. And if one were to count the early period, the library was now forty-four years old. Yet, with the exception of Mr. Whitehead (deceased) the Club's honorary trustees, Mrs. Weyl and Florence Webster, were still active members of the library. Between the mid-thirties and 1957 three more names had been added to the list of honorary trustees: Victor Lasher; Alice Wardwell; and Louise Lindin.

During this same month the board learned of the death of its Librarian Emeritus, Alice Thompson. In her letter to Mrs. Schrader, Mrs. Thompson's daughter, the secretary said: "All of the Trustees wish to express to you and your sister their sympathies in the great personal loss you have sustained. Your mother was someone whom the whole community will remember in fondness and admiration for a long time to come."

Close on the heels of this sobering news came word that Georgia Lingafelt was seriously ill and would be unable to continue as chairman of the Book Committee, whereupon Alf Evers volunteered to be acting chairman "temporarily." The board expressed its gratitude, and so did Mrs. Wells despite the fact that she frequently found his scribbled notes difficult to decipher.

March, with its bitter cold nights and bone-chilling days, held small promise of spring; nevertheless the Membership Committee was already at work on material for its April fund-raising project. And this year it had come up with something that had never before been tried — a newsletter, no less.

Printed on one side of a letter-size pink sheet of paper, the feature article was headed: "Woodstock Library Launches Its Annual Membership Drive."

Many of those who see that the Library is open to all those living in Woodstock, do not realize that it is not a public tax-supported institution but a membership organization receiving less than ten per cent from public money. . . . Our Library is not controlled by officials in Albany or Kingston or anywhere else but by its own members right here in Woodstock. . . . So the more members we have the greater will be the guarantee that the Library will be exactly the kind of institution the people of Woodstock need and want.

Lest this give the impression that the library intended to make its own laws and regulations rather than follow those under which it was chartered, we hasten to add that the writer of the article, President Laws, had her wires crossed.

The story in the next column could not have been written if the Woodstock Club's minutes had been available or if any of its charter members had been interviewed. It begins as follows:

The growth of the Woodstock Library from 1910 when Librarian Bruce Herrick presided over the Library's initial stock of a few hundred books makes a remarkable success story. Beginning in rented space in the Nook the Library took less than twenty years to grow big enough to fill the old part of its present building. Woodstock people sat up and took notice in 1930 when it was announced that the Library had circulated about 5,000 books that year. . . .

The wild guess that Bruce Herrick had started the Woodstock Library was accepted at face value. As for "the rented space in the Nook" that too was guesswork. In 1910 the so-called Nook was in fact an empty barn which would presently be purchased by George Neher and remodeled by him to house the Woodstock Club.*

But this was only the beginning. As circulation continued to amount and the Library's stock of books to grow bigger and bigger a fine new fireproof addition was built. . . .

"Fireproof?" Well, not exactly!

The third news item on this pink sheet was probably written by Alf Evers. It is headed: "Woodstock Library Once Pioneer Doctor's Home."

Built about a century and a half ago it served as the home and office of Dr. Larry Gilbert Hall who was probably the first doctor to settle down [in Woodstock] . . . delivering babies, prescribing for chills and fever and setting broken bones. Dr. Hall must have been a good physician for he was an early member of the county Medical Society, subscribed to medical journals, bought medical books and showed in a surviving record book of his that he kept up-to-date in advances in medical practice. About 1832 he built the one-story addition to the old part of [what is now] the Library and tradition says that each of the [eighteen] cut-out stars which decorate it represents one of the States then in the Union. An inventory of the doctor's estate shows by its inclusion of farming equipment that the doctor farmed on the side and it lists a "bathing trough" which may have been Woodstock's first bathtub.

As a postscript to the above account, here is a little more about the front of the library's so-called Ell — the entrance to the doctor's office, still unchanged. In addition to its cut-out stars in the board that forms the cornice, the good doctor further decorated the front of the building by adding the

---

* The writer, it seems, had read *The Wasp,* a local publication. The lead article in the August 2, 1952 issue is headed "A *Short History of The Woodstock Library.*" It is a masterpiece of misinformation. For example: "The Library was first [1910] located in the Nook and subsequently, as business in the Nook picked up and crowded out the books, in a small studio in the rear. . . ."

four pilasters which extend an inch or so from the wall. And for making and attaching the rectangular pillars, complete with capital and base, he paid Henry Davis three dollars for the three days' work. On the door itself is the original brass eagle knocker bearing Dr. Hall's name.

39

The Brook Goes Underground;
Another Memorial Fund

Victor Lasher's reluctance to part with the big field in front of the library had the trustees puzzled. Later he said by way of explanation that as long as he owned the land he had no drainage problem. "But if the library is willing to go to the additional expense of buying a large drain pipe," he told Mr. Dendy, "I'm ready to sell. But it must be stated in the contract that no structure — other than one for library purposes — may be built there as long as my wife or I occupy this house. . . ."

Before making his report at the May meeting (1957), Mr. Dendy had inquired into what the "additional expense" would amount to. "The corrugated, twenty-four inch, fourteen-gauge pipe specified would cost us about $1,250," he said, "and about $200 more for fill to cover it. As you know we have agreed to pay $3,000 for the land so the total will be approximately $4,450 — but I consider it a necessary investment." (The amount of the fill had been underestimated: an area 50 feet wide and 100 feet long from Mr. Lasher's land to Library Lane required so much fill that the cost came to $490.)

When put to vote, twelve trustees were in favor of the deal, one against, and one abstained.

The formal contract of sale reached Mrs. Laws in time for her to report on it at the members' meeting in June. "Mr. Dendy had read it carefully," she said, "and was quick to spot a discrepancy in the wording of the restrictions. He had pointed out that in the original agreement structures could be put up for *Library* purposes only, but this had been changed to 'no building or structures of any kind' as long as the Lashers *owned* or occupied any of the premises. However, we feel sure this can be rectified and Mr. Dendy recommends signing the contract with the changes noted."

In order to keep the membership informed on the rate the library had been growing, Mrs. Laws had worked out a table comparing the year 1953 with that of 1956 and this is the way it appears in the minutes:

	1953	1956	
Circulation	23,534	32,836	39%
New Books	477	1,055	220%
Spent on Books	$ 860	$1,545	180%
Budget	$6,036	$9,016	50%

Impressive indeed! But Mrs. Laws inadvertently conveyed a distorted picture when she compared the number of new books purchased in 1953 with the number purchased in 1956. What she had overlooked was the fact that from mid-May (1953) to the first of November, Mrs. Thompson was on sick leave and relatively few books were ordered before Mrs. Wells became librarian.

Having served three consecutive terms as president — a record in itself — Mrs. Laws had refused re-election. Upon receiving the chairman's gavel from her, Hilde Cohn, her successor, called upon Anita Smith, who then presented Jane Laws with an engraved silver plate as a token of the trustees' appreciation of her "tremendous contribution to the welfare and development of the Library."

In June, Arthur E. Hansen succeeded W. W. Blelock, Jr., as treasurer and like every former treasurer, Mr. Hansen's reports listed in detail, down to the last cent, all receipts and expenditures. His report at the August meeting gave the net returns from the Fair as $6,621.57. Probably no one who attended the Fair of 1958 will ever forget the violent and continuous rainstorm that curtailed business, cutting the profit that day to about $5,724. A sale held the following Saturday added $897.57, bringing the total to the figure in Mr. Hansen's report — just $987 less than the previous year. The president, Hilde Cohn, "introduced Mmes. [Inger] Walker," the entry reads, "and [Virginia] Anderson who were given a standing vote of thanks for their splendid work on behalf of the Fair. They reported as chairmen of the Fair and Great Expectations Committee respectively." Later, when the trustees were discussing plans for future Fairs, one of them wondered aloud if it might not be a good idea to purchase nylon tents to cover the entire Fair area.

Mr. Lasher's large drain pipe was not installed until after the Fair and the trustees who had been keeping an eye on the work reported at the September meeting that the closing off of the brook might create a serious drainage problem for the library. During downpours in the past, water had drained into the brook; what could be done to avoid having a pool of water collect on the parking lot? "It was decided to consult Mr. Cashdollar and Mr. Lasher," the entry in the minutes reads, an entry that may give the mistaken impression that a solution to the problem lay just around the corner.

The following month, in August, when the trustees learned of Georgia Lingafelt's death, they were saddened but thankful (since she could not recover) that her tragic illness had terminated. In a letter to the secretary, Ruth Lee, long a close friend of Miss Lingafelt, wrote: "A number of her friends both here and elsewhere . . . knowing how much she cared about the Library, have contributed to a fund to be spent at the discretion of the Board, the Book Committee and the Librarian. . . ."

At the close of 1957, under the heading Memorial Funds, the treasurer's report read:

Katherine Cleveland Fund
Balance 12/1/57	$235.00
Donations during year	95.00
Expenditure during year	249.25
Balance 12/31/57	$ 80.75

Georgia Lingafelt Fund
Donations during year	$275
Expenditures during year	50
Balance 12/31/57	$225

The budget for the coming year included two welcome increases. The town had increased its annual contribution by $100 and the Woodstock school had raised its by $90. The library's receipts were expected to exceed expenditures by the handsome sum of $744!

1.	School	$240
2.	Town	700
3.	State Library	100
4.	Fines	250
5.	Membership	1500
6.	Library Fair	7900

Receipts — $10,690   Disbursements — $9,946   Balance — $744

40

Book Borrowers and Bequests

On the evening of March 13, 1958, despite blustering winds and hazardous driving, by quarter past eight the Executive Committee, seated at the large round table in the wing, was ready for business as usual. This time, however, a guest was present: the Consultant from the Extension Division of the State Library — a Miss Gustafson. After being introduced by President Cohn, the lady from Albany talked about a plan in the making — "a plan which has the support of the Library Trustees' Foundation and which provides for pooling of resources among groups of libraries with a hundred-thousand-volume central library to serve as a reference source. . . ."

The Committee listened attentively; then one of its members asked how the proposed plan would affect Ulster County and Woodstock in particular.

"I will see that your Committee receives material on Library Laws regarding Municipal support and other problems," Miss Gustafson said reassuringly. So, for the time being, the matter was left in mid-air.

A challenging problem that cropped up every spring without fail turned out, in 1958, to be delightfully simple: the Membership Committee decided to use a slightly revised issue of Alf Evers' attractive brochure of 1955; and for the cover another photograph by Konrad Cramer — the one showing the front of the library framed by the sunlit foliage of the towering elm and two huge maples.

The response was impressive. In little over a month from the time the brochure was mailed, $1,251 had been received from 316 subscribers. A welcome sum but a shockingly small number of persons willing to be listed as "members" and this in a town with a population close to 4000. Not that only 316 readers used the library — far from it. Out of 1,370 registered borrowers (many with family cards), exactly 1,054 enjoyed all the services of the library without contributing one cent. Why?

Undoubtedly a large number of Woodstockers simply took their public library for granted — a place where one could get books of all kinds for the asking. True, but that was only one side of the coin; on the other, the design was as different as night from day.

If the town of Woodstock had ever been willing to donate more than a mere fraction (compare $700 with the 1958 budget of $10,690), no pleas for donations would have been necessary. But that was not the case. Those who withdrew books were served by a well-trained, paid staff, but behind that front was a small army of volunteers who kept the library going. Not because they had time on their hands and were looking for "something to do." They were the auxiliary crew that worked long hours but received no favors in return: they paid their annual dues, they paid the fine for books not returned on the specified date, etc., etc. Why did they contribute so much of their time to the needs of the library? Because they knew that if there were no behind-the-scenes volunteers, the Woodstock Library would fold. The instant it failed to pay its bills its charter would be revoked.

Did it *have* to have a charter? In pre-charter days the town refused to donate anything whatever, so did the State and the school. Without its charter it would have had to pay taxes to the town. It would eventually become (if anything) a rental library with a charge for books *by the day*.

The volunteers were a dedicated group. Understandably,

however, they would have been glad indeed if more of those who used the library had dug below the hole in their pocket and contributed at least the minimum membership fee each year. But wait — there was a way readers who did not care to pay anything could have had their cake and eaten it too. They could have banded together and convinced the Town Board that the Woodstock Library should be *fully tax supported.*

In the early spring, only a few weeks after the March meeting, the trustees were shocked by the sudden death of a fellow member, Lois Wilcox. A painter and retired art instructor, Miss Wilcox had a few years earlier purchased the rundown red barn on the corner of Glasco Turnpike and Rock City Road. Then with great skill and very little money she had converted the barn into a charming studio with living quarters. Because of her high regard for the library she had bequeathed the contents of the place to the library "to be disposed of as the Board saw fit."

This welcome leeway on Miss Wilcox's part enabled the board to hold a private sale in her studio, thus giving her friends first chance at her personal belongings — the rugs, chairs, and household effects. This produced about $325 for the library. The unsold articles — easels, artist's materials, frames, and a few paintings by Miss Wilcox — brought in about the same amount the day of the Fair and this, together with a $35 contribution in her name by her niece, amounted to a total of about $650. Of this sum $329.50 was earmarked by the board for the Wilcox Memorial Fund and the balance was set aside to be used "as needed." One of the current needs was a card catalog for the children's room and since Miss Wilcox had been especially interested in children's books and young readers, it was thought that such an addition to the library would undoubtedly have pleased her.

Meanwhile, the long-hoped-for drinking fountain, which

had been installed close to the library's small side porch, delighted the children. What no one had anticipated, however, was that trouble-makers would wrench off the long copper overflow pipe. It could not have been for the sake of turning a small profit — the broken pipe was left on the ground. Fortunately, the cost of replacing it with a length of galvanized iron pipe, instead of copper, was covered by insurance.

One item in the minutes of the September meeting catches the eye: "Albert Holumzer not only painted the floor of Mrs. Wells's office and gave the front porch two good coats of paint, but he did this on his own time and also supplied the paint. The Library is indeed grateful to this public-spirited citizen."

PART FOUR : 1959-1972

41

Proposed Library System Gains Momentum; The Oxhandler Fund

From library minutes dated October 9, 1959, we learn that President Hilde Cohn, accompanied by Lynn Wells, had attended a meeting of Orange, Sullivan, and Ulster Counties "to discuss the proposed plan for a Mid-Hudson Valley library system." No mention of where the meeting was held, but evidently both ladies were favorably impressed by what the plan had to offer.

Mrs. Cohn explained that the local affairs of each library would remain exactly as before joining the proposed system — each would continue to be responsible for raising its own funds as in the past. But the services to be gained by becoming a member would include a truck, on regular schedule, that would make deliveries and pick-ups of all kinds of books, recordings, and films. Routine work, such as cataloging and purchasing of books, she said, could be done in a central headquarters office, thus saving time and money for everyone.

"Mrs. Cohn was authorized to fill out and return a preliminary questionnaire," the secretary wrote, "and to state that Kingston would be our preference as to location for the Bureau."

One of the duties of the Planning Committee of the new system was to find places in which to hold meetings and the Woodstock Library, it seems, was high on the list. In a letter addressed to President Cohn, dated October 25, 1958, the co-chairman of the Committee, Mrs. Gerald Carson, wrote: "I am delighted that you can arrange an area meeting for 45 persons in December . . . I think a dinner after the meetings would be an excellent opportunity for people to mingle and get better acquainted, Dutch Treat, of course. . . ."

After a further exchange of letters between the two, the date for the meeting was set: December 13, 1958 at 2:30 p.m. In her letter of invitation, presumably mailed to all libraries in the three-county area, Mrs. Cohn urged members and trustees to attend because "this meeting may be of great importance to all of us. . . ."

Even so, when writing the minutes of the library's November and December meetings the secretary had nothing whatever to say about the special meeting held on the 13th. One of the trustees, however, remembers that the subject of a three-county versus a five-county system was discussed and that many of those present considered the latter preferable. "Mrs. Carson was one of the speakers," she recalled, "and tea was served."

In January (1959) a letter from Mrs. Carson created a minor storm. Without inquiring in advance how the trustees would feel about it, she wrote that the Planning Board of the new Library System was considering the possibility of making the Woodstock Library "a subsidiary reference station within the 5-county system."

For those who had been working for years to build the library into the type of library it was, with its fine collection of art books largely purchased with Memorial Funds, the very thought of having it converted into a reference center, to be overrun by hordes of out-of-towners, was enough to make hackles rise. Certain of the trustees took an over-my-dead-body stance. Fortunately nothing came of the proposal; it was only one of the many suggestions under consideration.

The annual meeting, with Acting-President Evers in the chair, was held on June 11. He began his report by expressing deep regret over the resignation of Mrs. Cohn as president and trustee:

"This year has been marked by a loss to the Community which has had an effect on the administration of the Library. The long illness and eventual death of Dr. Hans Cohn who had become so valuable a part of Woodstock life as doctor, musician and public-spirited citizen made it necessary for his wife Hilde to turn over the duties of Library President, which she had carried on so well, to the Vice-President. . . ." After giving Mrs. Cohn credit for what she had accomplished in exploring "a new and important development whose aim it was to bring the people of New York a far higher standard of library service than they now have," Mr. Evers went on to speak of other systems. "There are many now in operation elsewhere in the State. We too can have access to a reference library of over a hundred thousand volumes [the location still undetermined], a greater economy in purchasing and processing books, the advantage of a corps of professional libraries to advise and assist our own and many other advantages without giving up in any way the individuality and freedom of choice and action of our own Library. . . . It should be stressed that our Library is under no obligation to join such an association. But if the advantages which have come to the members of other such systems seem likely to follow joining the one now being sketched out, I believe we should join without hesitation."

The fact that their fellow-member Alf wanted the library to join the new system carried considerable weight with the trustees. Actually there was no longer much doubt as to which way the wind was blowing.

At the board meeting, held after the members had departed, the following slate of officers was elected for the coming term: president, Alf Evers; vice-president, Arthur Hansen; secretary, Margot (Mrs. Gordon) Taylor; treasurer, Harris Gordon, a comparative newcomer.

Although her friends had known that Rose Oxhandler had been ill for a long time, few of them were prepared for the news of her untimely death shortly after the library meeting in June. When word spread that a memorial fund was being established, contributions poured in at an impressive rate, with some of the envelopes bearing such far-off postmarks as San Antonio, Texas. When the Executive Committee met in July, Mr. Evers reported that two of the contributors had made an unusual request: that a bluestone plaque be placed in the library in memory of Mrs. Oxhandler. But this was not in keeping with library policy. After a lengthy discussion of what to do in lieu of a bluestone plaque, the subject was temporarily tabled.

The Fair that summer took in the heart-warming gross of $9,115.47, but the prizes for Great Expectations and other expenses took a big cut out of the total, reducing it to a net of $7,121.52.

As one sage remarked at the time, "You've got to spend money to make money."

Alf Evers was as busy with his own affairs as the next person; nevertheless, in September he accepted the chairmanship of the Mid-Hudson's Steering Committee. He also made a valiant effort to convince the Town Board that it should up its contribution to the library from $700 to $1000, pointing out that the estimated budget for 1960 would be close to $10,000 — the highest in its history. The town fathers were not impressed with Mr. Evers' well-phrased appeal but they were willing to inch the appropriation up a little: they voted to allow the library $800 for the coming year. President Evers' strong plea in behalf of the library did cause the Onteora Board of Education (but not without considerable backing and filling on its part) to continue its donation of $250.

All in all it had been a good year, but for President Evers "it was the coming into being of the Mid-Hudson Libaries that was of outstanding importance." Much of his report at the annual meeting in June 1960 was devoted to an explanation of how much would be gained by the Woodstock Library now that it had become a member, at the end of 1959, of the five-county co-operative system. He stressed the importance of the Central Reference Library. "Before long our librarian will need only make a collect telephone call to have any book from its great stock reach Woodstock usually within twenty-four hours. . . . Rotating collections of books of fiction, or on any such subject as science, history or gardening bought from System funds will move from library to library and when they have made the rounds will be shared among individual libraries of the system and come to rest on their shelves. Good collections of records, films, and local historical materials will be available for loan to member libraries. . . ."

It was a stimulating speech and was accepted with enthusiastic applause.

42

More Storage Space; The Parking Place; The Tree Trust

The new president, Arthur Hansen, personally shouldered the heavy burden of running the Fair in 1960 and while it proved to be larger and better attended than ever before, it did not do much better financially (as had been expected) than previous Fairs — netting only $7,420.17.

"There was a discussion of some of the problems inherent in staging the Fair," the minutes state, "including the difficulties of getting adequate help to handle the job. It is thought the saturation point has been reached and it would be wise to concentrate on quality rather than quantity. . . . Mr. Hansen said that administration of the Fair had been complicated by inadequacies of the Fair Building."

In other words, more storage space was needed, especially for the hundreds of books that accumulated between Fairs. The board was in full agreement, so during the next few months a committee, headed by Mr. Hansen, studied every aspect of a plan to enlarge the storage space by adding a room between the north wall of the wing and the south side of the Fair Building. When the plan was submitted, together with a drawing by John Pike, the president called attention to the library's need for indoor public toilets. By extending the southwest corner of the children's room, he said, it would be possible to install two toilets with a single entrance.

The plan was accepted with the proviso that the cost would not exceed $5,000. So the committee cut corners wherever possible and despite an unusually wet spring, the new book-storage room and the structure (with public toilets) added to the corner of the children's room were ready in time for the Fair in the summer of 1961. The cost had exceeded the ceiling set by the board but was not questioned, nor did anyone ask if the old drainage system (presumably installed in 1948) had been enlarged.

One problem that had continued to haunt the library year in and year out was the condition of the parking place. "Don't the trustees *know* about all the mud puddles?" indignant patrons would demand of Mrs. Wells. "Why don't they *do* something about it?"

Why, indeed? The chairman of Administration had warned the board that if the town carried out its plan to raise the level of Library Lane by a foot or more, the parking lot would have a lake along its entrance. And when the town fathers failed to respond to the library's plea for help, the new secretary, Janette Steinlauf, a Vassar graduate with a head for business, wrote to the head of the New York State Department of Public Works. She called the Commission's attention to the streams of water which run off the State road at the intersection of the Library Lane down to the parking lot. "Water is a mere nuisance during the summer but when its freezes in sheets in the winter months a grave hazard exists. The Board of the Library is concerned lest some patron sustain serious injuries from a fall. . . ."

It was a good try but the answer to this letter (and there probably was one) may not have been considered of enough importance to be mentioned in the minutes.

In the meantime a small flurry of indignation swept the board. It was caused by the publication of the handsome, illustrated bulletin distributed by the Woodstock Tree Trust in cooperation with "a militant group of citizens who feel strongly about the importance of trees in the life and future of Woodstock."

The board felt as strongly as did the "militant group" about the importance of trees, but what had disturbed the trustees was the picture in the bulletin of the tree being removed near the entrance of the library. Although it was still upright, there was a large V-shaped cut extending part way through the trunk, and the caption under the picture pointed an accusing finger at the library trustees. In capital letters it ran as follows:

THIS BIG MAPLE GREETED US UPON ENTERING THE FAMED WOODSTOCK LIBRARY . . . UNTIL IT FELL TO THE AX IN APRIL. WE COUNTED 80 YEAR RINGS. PROPER CARE IN ITS EARLIER YEARS COULD HAVE EXTENDED ITS LIFE FOR A GENERATION.

Determined to set the record straight, the Executive Committee directed the secretary to write to the head of the Tree Trust and a copy of her letter, with the reply she received by return mail are on file. After an expression of sympathy for the aims of the Tree Trust, Mrs. Steinlauf continued, "However, in all fairness to the Library Administration, and in the interests of accuracy, if nothing else, the Trustees of the Library would like to point out that 'the big maple' . . . was a black locust tree, anywhere from 130–160 years old, one of the six original locusts purchased by Dr. Larry Hall to shade his doorway. Although locust trees have a habit of lasting well over a hundred years . . . this particular tree had suffered a serious injury, probably by lightning, at some early time. But for the past 14 years or so the Library Administration has exercised caution and care in managing the trees on the Library property. In the case of this tree, both Mr. Cedric Newton and Mr. Peter Foskett were consulted and determined that a tree of such age and unsound condition posed a threat to Library patrons and the Library building, standing as it did directly at the entrance. In some less public location it might have been feasible to treat and wait!

"Anyone not familiar with Library tree policy, reading the text of the tree bulletin might jump to the conclusion that the Administration had callously and wantonly chopped down a tree which had not only been mistreated and neglected but might have lived another generation or so. Actually, long months before the bulletin was published the Administration and Library Board had been discussing long range plans to prolong the life and beauty of Library trees and to formulate a replacement plan which would not exhaust the budget."

The reply, addressed to Mrs. Steinlauf, admitted that the "Woodstock Tree Trust deserves every bit of criticism you bring forth, and that comes 100% on my head for writing this text. Just as an explanation and not as an excuse: I needed an example of a recently cut tree of public interest, and assumed too much — should have checked carefully before picking on this one. . . . I assure you I shall use the first opportunity to apologize publicly in print and remove any inferred criticism, which was not intended but may have crept in. My sincere apologies and also my congratulations for the beautiful way things are kept around the Library. Sincerely, J. Constant van Rijn, Temporarily in charge for Woodstock Tree Trust."

It was a handsome apology, and peace was restored.

43

The Death of a Founder; A Welcome Fluke; The Drainage Field

January 1961 was the coldest, the darkest, the snowiest month in recent years. Even the MHL *Newsletter* began in capital letters: "SNOW, SNOW AND MORE SNOW . . . that has been the story. System trustees' meetings for December and January were cancelled because of snowstorms and sub-zero weather. . . ."

Not so in Woodstock: the Executive Committee braved the weather and met as usual. It must be admitted, however, that the minutes of the January meeting were unusually short and those recorded in February even shorter.

News of Mrs. Weyl's death in Washington in March reached the Library in a letter from her friend, Mari Boll-man, to Anita Smith, and the entry in the minutes reads: "Re-solved, that we express to her family our deep regret and sense of loss in her passing with the comforting knowledge that her friendly manner and wise counsel will always be gratefully remembered."

Mrs. Weyl's generosity in providing the fledgling library with a building of its own was well known, but it was not un-til the April meeting that the board learned that "Honorary Trustee Bertha Weyl had remembered the library in her will, leaving the sum of $1,000 for the purchase of books." In mak-ing the announcement Mr. Hansen said that the money had been placed in a Memorial Fund together with a gift in her memory from Mr. and Mrs. Adrian Siegel of Philadelphia, but did not state the amount donated. Furthermore, her son, Nathaniel, "has made a most generous gift of 1981 books comprising Mrs. Weyl's library in Woodstock.'

In April, the library received a form letter from the MHL that was so amazing that it was like a dream come true. It began:

"To Librarians of the Member Libraries,
"As an enclosure, we are sending you a check in payment of the Item 4 matching grant.
"This money, under the terms of the grant, must be spent for books, periodicals or binding.
"You, of course, will determine the rate at which you wish to spend it, but it must be spent in 1961. I should suggest that you plan to have obligated this money by October 1, 1961, at the latest so you can be certain that all of the books will have arrived and been paid for before the end of the calendar year 1961. . . ."

Not a word about the size of the check enclosed, but at the top of the letter in the treasurer's handwriting we find this: "Check $2,098.01 Deposited 4-19-61."

Could the Book Committee spend more than $2,000 for books in a matter of months? Easily and with gusto. In her letter of acknowledgement, Janette Steinlauf wrote: "Speaking as a member of the Book Committee, it means a great deal to be able, at last, to fatten out the leaner sections which develop in every library. While the Woodstock Library is older and better stocked than many small libraries, we try to recognize weakness and it is a great satisfaction to have funds available for book purchases at this time."

Then like frosting on the cake, in July came another check, this time $2,000 "for your share of the funds distributed by the Onteora Schools to chartered libraries in the school district."

From the excellent report of its co-chairmen, "Ginger" Anderson and Margot Taylor, we learn that the Library Fair of 1961 opened at 11 a.m. on "our traditional Thursday to sunny skies, warm weather — and a tremendous crowd. . . . The net result was $7,650.02, over $100 more than last year, and while financially we can all feel the Fair was a success, there are many areas which need improvement — and change.

"Volunteer help, especially male help, has become increasingly difficult to obtain. Every organization in town has felt this and the Fair, coming at the height of the vacation season as it does, is acutely affected. Our first recommendation is that we again attempt to contract for the physical setup of the Fair grounds . . . the setting up of the tables, moving of merchandise, etc. would be done by the contracting firm. This would be a very worthwhile expense in the long run — we're 'killing' some of our strongest helpers. . . . There were two new features of the Fair this year — an Antique Table which was almost completely sold out by 3 p.m. The best and most unique items were kept for this table, proving that the public is interested and will pay for quality. [The second feature] was ice cream on a concession basis which took little space and pleased everyone. . . . Suggestions [for future Fairs]: doing the Library Fair on a lesser scale, preceded earlier in the summer by an auction; perhaps a separate book sale; a thrift shop maintained in the name of the Library, using the Collection Center every Saturday; elimination of the Fair and having an auction at one time, a Book Sale later. . . ."

Sixteen of the trustees dutifully showed up at the September meeting; President Hansen had hoped for a larger attendance since there was a guest speaker, Harold O. Harlan of the MHL. Mr. Harlan sat patiently through the reading of the minutes of the previous meeting and the treasurer's report but if one could judge by the expression on his face, he found what the librarian had to say of greater interest. Mrs. Wells spoke of the gain in circulation figures in August —

5,150 as against 4,690 in August 1960. "This means," she said, "the three of us handled 10,300 books on an in-out basis during a single month."

After further reports the president introduced the Director of the Mid-Hudson Library System who spoke of the pioneer aspects of the new system, of the forty-three libraries presently involved serving 376,000 people in five counties. He then enlarged on the advantages of the "exchange program" and "interlibrary loans. . . ."

One member who had been on the Book Committee longer than anyone else could scarcely wait until the close of his address to raise her hand, indicating that she wished to speak. As soon as the president recognized Miss Doughty she said a little breathlessly: "'If our rare art books are not lendable to the Woodstock population, it would scarcely seem proper to loan them through the system."

Mr. Harlan agreed. Each library was free to make its own rules, he said.

Next, Mrs. Steinlauf with the $2,098.01 check in mind, asked just what could be expected in the future in the way of grants to member libraries. This was not a welcome question but Mr. Harlan did not evade it. The out-sized grant last time was a "fluke," he said; libraries could expect no more than $250 in the future, usable only for books.

The final entry in the minutes that day recorded "a discussion of methods of raising money to expand the present building in Woodstock." Once again the board was wondering how it could find additional space to house its growing collection of books.

By September the poor condition of the parking space could no longer be ignored so when President Hansen proposed a solution to the problem it was gladly accepted by the Executive Committee. He said that Bob Holsapple was now surfacing the Laundromat's parking area with blacktop and was willing to do the Library's for three hundred dollars. What's more, he would guarantee no more puddles because the water would drain off toward the library lawn.

"No more puddles!" The vote to accept Holsapple's guarantee was unanimous. Not long after the job was completed, however, low spots in the new surface held rain water even more efficiently than had the shale. And when these were pointed out to Mr. Holsapple he readily agreed to fill in the hollows "next spring." True to his word, he tried valiantly to patch the surface but after every rainfall two or more reflecting pools of water glistened in the wet blacktop. Finally he agreed to forfeit his final payment; shale was spread as a top dressing over the blacktop, and for the rest of the year there were no more puddles.

Even so, the library soon had another water problem to cope with. A rather cryptic entry in the minutes reads: "Unfortunately, the septic tank again overflowed . . . it is apparent the drainage field must be properly enlarged in such a way to avoid interfering with the runoff pipe from the Lasher property."

When, for the first time, during the Fair of 1960, smelly water seeped up from below to collect around the tables, boards were spread to serve as stepping stones, and it was assumed that the newly installed public toilets had flooded the septic tank. Later when someone discovered a metal bottle cap in the water tank of the men's toilet the reaction was: "That explains it! The cap held the valve open and the continuous flow flooded the septic tank — it won't happen again."

But it did (as noted in the minutes), and the committee appointed to arrange for a "properly enlarged" drainage field engaged William West, Sr., whose contract price for the job was $1,000. The chairman of Administration clearly remembers the day when Mr. West asked her to "come and take a look at what we've uncovered." There, in place of the septic tank supposedly installed in 1948, was a deep hole — no tank, no drainage field.

The new large, well-constructed drainage field solved that problem for the library but the other one — the lack of drainage in the parking space — remained as troublesome as ever. Finally, the yearly loads of shale brought the level of the area up to approximately that of Library Lane and when, thanks to William Klementis' roadmen, a narrow ditch was dug along the edge of the road, the rain water drained off into the low grassy hollow beside the parking space — at best, a temporary solution.

44

Memorial Monies; A Strip of Land;
The Failure to Qualify

As long as anyone could remember, the "year" for the library's officers had begun in June. At the session following the members' meeting the retiring officers either stepped down or, if willing, continued on for another term. In June of 1962 President Hansen was succeeded by Margot Taylor; Janette Steinlauf became vice-president; Virginia Anderson took on the difficult task of treasurer; and a recently elected member of the board, Jane (Mrs. Manuel) Bromberg became secretary. From here on, for the remainder of the 1962–63 term, there are wide gaps in the record because most of Mrs. Bromberg's minutes — loose-leaf sheets in longhand — are missing.

Even so, it is known that the Fair that summer, under the energetic management of another comparatively new trustee, Nancy (Mrs. Percy) Lyon, did surprisingly well. This was due, in part, to two follow-up enterprises: a book sale ($193.19) and the auction ($977.65). When added to the Fair's net intake of $8,507.04 the grand total came to a new high — $9,677.88!

Another event that took place in 1962 is covered by a letter dated October 22. It begins: "Under the terms of Mr. Eugene Speicher's will it is expected that the Library will receive upwards of $4,000 to be used for the purchase of art books. . . ." The next paragraph in the letter gave everyone pause. Because the will was ambiguous, it stated, a quit claim would have to be signed by those concerned before the estate could be settled. There were further complications, however, and when the library received its first check it was for $2,000 — only half the amount hoped for. But eventually the difficulties were ironed out and in the spring of 1965 another check arrived bringing the total to $3,571. The check was promptly deposited by the treasurer under the heading "general account."

The Book Committee blithely continued to order fine art books and charge them to the Speicher Memorial Fund and it did not seem to occur to any of the trustees that because the treasurers had long since stopped keeping a separate record of what was being spent from the Memorial Funds, there was no way of telling how much remained in each of the various Funds.

Another substantial sum, the Rose Oxhandler Memorial Money, had also been banked under the same heading. It had taken the Executive Committee some time to reach a decision on how best to use the money contributed in her memory. When the Committee had finally decided to purchase a handsomely bound book to be dedicated to Rose Oxhandler, there was another long delay because, as it turned out, it was not easy to locate an "illuminator" to letter the text. According to plan, it would open with a short history of the library and this would be followed "by a page for every person who had left something to the Library." But who would supply the information? Next to nothing was known, at that time, about the early days of the library, and even less about donors long dead. Even before an illustrator was found who would be willing to do the extensive hand lettering for a reasonable sum, the Executive Committee was puzzling over how such a book could be displayed. One proposal called for it to be placed under glass "to prevent its being handled and soiled."

Finally the Committee reached the sensible conclusion to use the money for books purchased in memory of Rose Oxhandler. And with that, the $498 became part of the library's savings account.

This offhand method of bookkeeping greatly disturbed

Mari Bollman, who had become the chairman of the Book Committee in 1962. She pointed out that when a bequest specified that the money should be used for books, not to comply was illegal. Furthermore, *all* Memorial Funds earmarked for books, she said, should be kept in a separate account.

Did the library turn over a new leaf and revise its method of bookkeeping? Strangely enough the answer is no, but the reason may have been that with each passing year the treasurer's job had become ever more complicated. At any rate, it was not until much later, when Miss Bollman again introduced the subject, that the trustees took the matter seriously. They not only agreed with her but appointed her Administrator of Memorial Funds. From the scant information available she managed to bring the record up to date and from then on in her reports not an *i* was left undotted, not a *t* went uncrossed.

In the winter of 1962–63, the board learned that Victor Lasher was willing to sell the long narrow strip of land bordering Tannery Brook. Located directly across the road from the library property it had been used in recent years for extra tables during the annual Fairs, and while quite a number of trustees were in favor of buying the strip, they questioned Mr. Lasher's price: $1500. When Margot Taylor discussed the matter with him he did agree to reduce his asking price to $1000, but even at that the amount seemed unduly high since the land would be used by the Fair only one day in the year. It was Alvin Moscowitz who introduced a practical note when he quoted a member of the Chamber of Commerce. "He said that in *his* opinion since the land could not be used for building it was not worth more than $500." It was common knowledge that Gordon Anderson wanted the strip because of his "water rights" — whatever that meant. And since the board realized that sooner or later the library building would have to be enlarged in order to house its growing collection, it voted against using its savings for the purchase of the narrow strip of land.

Filed with the records of 1963 is an announcement that the Book of the Month Club was offering substantial cash awards to libraries throughout the country in memory of Dorothy Canfield Fisher. With understandable pride in what the Woodstock Library had accomplished during the past fifty years, a letter of application was written tracing its development from a one-room collection operating on a shoestring to its present status which was, according to headquarters in Albany, "one of the best libraries of its kind for a town of its size in the entire State." The letter was signed by President Margot Taylor and sent hopefully on its way. Later on, after the names of the winners of the awards had been announced, the trustees learned that the Woodstock Library had not been considered eligible. So one of the first things Janette Steinlauf did, after succeeding Margot Taylor in June as president, was to write to Mr. Goldenson, Director of the Library awards, to request that he clarify certain paragraphs in the application because otherwise "quite possibly we would never know precisely why we failed to qualify."

The answer from Mr. Goldenson's office left no doubt whatever as to why the Woodstock Library was not eligible:

". . . Criterion 5 does, I am afraid, mean tax funds. The funds may come from any governmental unit, state, county, school district, village, etc. but not from endowment income, the proceeds or raffles, individual donations, or community chest funds. There are two reasons for this: 1. experience has proved the country over, that the only reliable support for libraries over the long pull is tax monies; 2. since communities use their tax resources for what they consider most important, tax support is a measure of the community's interest and concern for the educational values of sound public libraries. . . ."

"The only reliable support for libraries over the long pull is tax monies. . . ." The trustees could wholeheartedly agree with that, but none of them could figure out a way to convince the town fathers that "support is a measure of the community's interest and concern. . . ."

45

Comfort Versus the Ornamental; A Saturday Fair; Public Monies

For the trustees the year 1964 proved to be a period in which quite a number of comparatively small yet important matters were handled in bits and pieces. For example, the replacement of the unique chairs that matched the long yellow table in the wing. Embedded in the top of the table is a brass plate bearing this legend: "Table and chairs made from Overlook Mountain timber, turned in Shady Mill and constructed by Iris Wolven. Gift of Victor and Eleanor Cannon."

Now, ornamental as the chairs undoubtedly were, those who had perched on them while reading always discovered how truly uncomfortable they could be. Well aware of this, the trustees had time and again discussed the matter of replacing them. Finally that bridge was crossed. Sixteen "Captain's chairs" costing $23.65 each (plus freight and delivery) were purchased, much to most readers' relief.

Another item of interest in 1964 was the return of ex-President Margot Taylor in June to serve a second term, succeeding Janette Steinlauf. Virginia Anderson, who had retired as treasurer, took over another exacting job, that of secretary. But the newsmaking event of the year was the Saturday Fair. Co-Chairmen Vern May and Michael Boyle had done such a splendid job of management that the Fair's gross intake had hit a new high: $11,308.99. Expenses, however, whittled that fine sum down to a net of $7,423.30.

During the board meeting in August, the trustees took a hard look at the question: Had anything been gained by holding the Fair on Saturday? It was known that the merchants greatly objected to the change. They said that it interfered with their weekend business, and that it diverted customers. Whereupon Mr. May pointed out that the library simply *had* to make all the money it could, therefore the Fair should be held on the day when it could draw the largest crowd. "Based on present estimates of tax funds," he went on, "including both town and central school monies, for every dollar received the library must raise four dollars and fifty cents." He felt that Saturday was a better Fair Day because everything had been sold out long before closing time; and that given good weather and more things to sell, future fairs could net as much as $10,000.

This brought a quick retort from ex-Fair chairman Nancy Lyon. "Even when held on Thursdays the Fairs have sold out before closing time," she said. She herself had found it difficult to locate women to work on weekends because of guests.

It may have been what Margot Taylor reported that carried the most weight. She had checked back as far as 1958 and had found that in every case Saturday was no improvement on Thursday. "The net returns were as high or even *higher* than this year."

When David Carlson moved that "next year's Fair be held on the last Thursday in July," the motion was carried — and that was that for the next six years.

The last entry in the minutes was headed "Building Plans." It stressed the need for space and possible methods of "expanding facilities. John Natoli agreed to serve as co-chairman with Miss Rogers to investigate this. Mr. West will also serve."

46

A Timely Bequest; New Ideas for the Fair

The resignation of Secretary Anderson in June of 1965 set the Nominating Committee to searching through its list of trustees and when no one could be found who was willing to take on the job, always a difficult post to fill, the chairman of the Book Committee, Mari Bollman, was asked to pinch-hit temporarily.

So, being the sort of person who, regardless of her own busy schedule, helps out in case of need, Miss Bollman accepted. It is the last paragraph of her three-page report of the July Executive Meeting that concerns us here. It reads: "The Library has received a copy of the will of Mabel Van Alstyne Marsh from Mr. LeFever's office in Kingston and a notification that 15% of the Residuary Estate is to be given to the Woodstock Library for enlarging the Library."

When the news of Mrs. Marsh's bequest had reached Frances Rogers, chairman of the Administration Committee, she had recalled one of the last conversations she had had with her friend, Mrs. Marsh, just prior to the serious illness that terminated in her death on July 4. The two had talked about the library and how much it meant to the town. "We're trying to figure out a way to enlarge the building," Miss Rogers had told her, "and one plan under consideration is cutting an opening from the wing into the book storage shed. . . ."

Mrs. Marsh had said little at the time — she was far from well — but the fact that shortly thereafter she had added a codicil to her will was significant. The original will had set up a foundation, a form of holding company, for various charitable purposes, but the codicil abolished the foundation and instead divided her residuary estate, including securities and her Woodstock property, a summer home on Ohayo Mountain, as follows:

> 50% to Rensselaer Polytechnic Institution
> 35% to the Kingston Hospital
> 15% to the Woodstock Library

In August a special meeting of the Executive Committee was called to clarify the position of the executors of the will, Mrs. Marsh's niece Betty Sheldon and a friend of long standing, Fred Johnston of Kingston. A question was put to them concerning the wording of the will. It stated that Mrs. Marsh "directs" that the money be used "for the enlargement of the Library." Did the word "enlargement" specify an addition to the building or did it include books and facilities?

"That is a legal point," the trustees were told, "to be decided by Mr. LeFever, Mrs. Marsh's lawyer." Mr. LeFever concluded that "enlargement meant building, not books." Meanwhile what Mr. Johnston wanted fully understood was that Mrs. Marsh's wishes were to be carried out, including those given by word of mouth. He then quoted her as having said that any addition to the building should conform to the Colonial style — nothing ultra-modern — and that she wanted Albert Milliken of Kingston to be the architect.

"There may be some question as to Mrs. Marsh's 1963 income tax," Mr. Johnston went on, "which could hold up the final settlement of the will: otherwise the Library might expect to receive the money next year. However, until the Woodstock property is sold and all claims adjusted, we shall not know the amount of the residuary estate."

Delighted at this happy turn of events, the committee of three (John Natoli, who had resigned, was succeeded by John Stefano) that had been striving to work out a way to enlarge the library at a minimal cost — the makeshift plan of converting the book storage shed into a room for additional stacks — gladly turned instead to consideration of library needs on a larger scale: increased space, better lighting, possibly a usable upper story. Then, as directed, they consulted Mr. Milliken.

With Mari Bollman serving as secretary *pro tem,* all the minutes during this period are impressively clear and complete. At the regular trustees' meeting in August, much time was devoted to the discussion of the 1965 Fair and suggestions for future Fairs. Here, then, is an excerpt from the entry as written:

"Anderson: Suggested that we can scarcely expect more than $8,000 gross in any coming year; we should think up additional ways to raise money — special book sales, auctions, entertainments, etc.

"Hansen: the Fair peters out after 3 p.m. We should open later; have the Fair some place else perhaps; have something other than the Fair; particularly stressed auctions.

"Mathews: Instead of Fair, have three different events, and suggested book sales and art auctions (all articles in an auction to be put up at a bottom, or starting, price.)

"Heerman [Norbert Heerman, artist and photographer]: Volunteered to contact Artists Association about artists donating pictures next year.

"Goldberg: There being so much stealing, the shopping bags should be ruled out for next year. Also, we need a stronger fence to keep the public out until opening time. Stressed the manpower shortage (in which all concurred), which made it impossible for one person at each table to watch the cash box. (Another reason for not having the Fair on a Thursday, or during Rotron's vacation.) One big failure was the Midway, because the adults to supervise it did not turn up, leaving it manned only by children who gave so much away that the Midway ended with a deficit.

"Stefano: Pointed out, as did others, that the Fair dies out by 3 p.m. Has heard remarks that the Fair always has the same old things — we need new, exciting things or activities — and suggested a committee to work out new ideas or think up new ways of raising money.

"West: As a committee of one, in past year, has asked many people for suggestions and they all thought that if the Library could raise about $7,000 net in one day, it 'had a good thing going' and couldn't suggest anything other than our Fair.

"Nevertheless, a committee was appointed, consisting of John Stefano as Chairman, Art Hansen, Ginger Anderson, Jane Keefe, and John Natoli, to consider all above suggestions, sift new ideas and plan next year's date and report at the September Trustees' Meeting for their decision. . . ."

Yet not a word appears in the minutes of the meeting in September about a report from the committee of five appointed to "sift new ideas." Nor in the minutes of October or November. Then in December the subject is covered in less than two typed lines: "Two new ideas for Fair Day were suggested: 'Silent auction' by Peter Rakov and 'Chinese auction' by John Stefano." All of which shows how very difficult it is, even for those who know all the ins and outs of staging a fair, to think up new ways of doing what has been done repeatedly in the past.

47

The Architect; A Resignation and the Search for a Replacement

It was not until March of 1966 that the Building Committee had an opportunity to meet with Mr. Milliken and show him through the library. "This is where we had planned to cut an opening into the book storage shed," Miss Rogers told him, indicating the north wall of the wing. After one quick glance the architect dismissed the idea. "It would be better to extend the *end* of the wing out toward the road," he said — a practical suggestion that had not occurred to any of the trustees.

One thing they did stress was that under no circumstances should the front of the old entrance to the Ell be changed — it was sufficiently Colonial in style as it was.

With plans fast taking shape before the board had learned how much the library would receive as its share of the Marsh estate, the idea of applying for a Federal grant for public library construction was given serious consideration. According to the "Criteria For Selection of Public Library Building Projects," presented by Peter Rakov, the Woodstock Library was eligible as a "small" library because it served less than 10,000 people; had an annual circulation of at least 30,000 last year; was located within two or three blocks of the center of town; was a member of a library system. Then came a clause with capital letters to emphasize its importance: "Such a library MUST HAVE AN ANNUAL INCOME OF $2.00 PER CAPITA, EXCLUDING capital expenditure."

Since the town's contribution of $1,200 was far short of

what that sum would be, the library did not stand a ghost of a chance and the trustees knew it.

By late September of 1966, however, much progress had been made: a check for $60,000 had been received from the Marsh estate; and the architect had submitted preliminary drawings that called for extensive remodeling of the old building in addition to the plan to enlarge it: by removing the existing front wall and constructing a new one (and entrance) some ten feet farther out; a new east wall six feet out toward Library Lane, and extending the end of the wing by sixteen feet, the architect said, considerably more space would be gained.

The practical-minded Mike Boyle pointed out the difficulties involved if the old structure in front had to be propped up while the two new walls were being built. He said he believed it would be better to raze the entire front room and start from the ground up. Everyone, including Mr. Milliken, agreed. When asked how early the work on the project could begin he had replied, "Not before April. And it should take three months." As for the cost, he believed it would amount to about $54,484 including his ten per cent fee — a figure well within the $60,000 bequest.

What came as a total surprise was librarian Lynn Wells's announcement that she planned to retire after the first of the year, in February to be exact, and when urged to stay on for at least another year, she said that her family was insisting that she quit while she could still enjoy life and go on a long cruise, possibly around the world.

"Lynn's resignation at this time," Secretary Carolyn Wilson wrote, "defeats further thought of attempting to keep the Library open during the three months of construction. Lynn offered to train a new person in cataloging but it was felt advisable to try to get someone with training."

Someone with training, willing to take a part-time job in the country at a salary the library could afford to pay.

Where, in heaven's name, could the trustees find such a person? No one, at the time, could offer a ray of hope.

It so happened, however, that not long thereafter Carolyn Wilson and her husband, Reginald, were dinner guests of the Richard Robertses at their home on Purdy Hollow Road in Zena, a place they used only for weekends and vacations. During the course of the conversation Mrs. Wilson asked, casually, why the two didn't — or when they would — live full time in Woodstock. The answer was simple and to the point: both the Robertses had — and needed — fulltime jobs. Ellin was a Senior Editor at Doubleday and Company in New York City; Richard, Senior Editor with Dell Publishing.

With the library opening in mind, Carolyn Wilson asked if Ellin had ever considered becoming a librarian and then went on to explain the circumstances.

Mrs. Roberts, amused, replied that such a thought had never entered her head. Amply supplied with books of their own, she and Richard had seldom even been in the Woodstock Library although they had contributed books. She knew nothing about running a library, she said, but it might be something to think about.

Intrigued by the possibility of having a person like Ellin as librarian — if the Robertses could by one means or another make Woodstock their headquarters — Carolyn Wilson reported that in her opinion Mrs. Roberts' qualifications, as to temperament, personality and general education "were perfect."

The response of the Committee is summed up in a short paragraph in the minutes: "Carolyn is to talk to Ellin and make an appointment for Saturday morning November 19 so that the rest of the Executive Committee may have the opportunity of meeting and talking with her."

Even so, that meeting did not take place in November and it was not until later, after Mrs. Roberts had met with a few members of the Executive Committee at Mrs. Wilson's home, that she began to consider the various possibilities and contingencies seriously.

In the meantime, the trustees were up to their ears in decision making: in addition to thrashing out endless details with the architect there was the question of how best to handle another bequest to the library — another windfall.

48

The Ives Bequest; A Small Party

The board listened with rapt attention while Alvin Moscowitz explained the will of the late Mrs. Alfred Ives. It stated that the contents of her home in Woodstock were to be sold at public auction in New York City and the net proceeds given to the library. Steps had already been taken to have the household effects appraised and one bid had been submitted. Barnfield would take a large part of the things — buy them outright for $30,000, transportation costs included.

What the board must decide, Mr. Moscowitz said, was whether or not to get a second appraisal. Possibly the Ives effects were worth considerably more than Mr. Barnfield's figure. Possibly an auction house like the Parke-Bernet Galleries would make a better offer.

The vote to get an appraisal from Parke-Bernet was unanimous and the entry in the minutes reads: "Meanwhile some members of the Library will go to see the Ives house, find out what Barnfield would take and what would be left for a so-called tag sale."

The Ives property, located part-way up the steeply winding Broadview Road, proved to be a showpiece from its very entrance, a garden filled to overflowing with massive ornamental stonework, stone steps leading up, up to the house high above. The interior of the house, too, gave the same impression — too much to see at too close range: museum pieces such as a large French commode, a Louis XVI table set with enamel portraits, Chinese paintings on glass, ornate bronze lions, Persian rugs galore. Barnfield's red tags were very much in evidence but gave no hint of the estimated value.

The report prepared by Parke-Bernet nipped all hope in the bud. The auction house would take only the cream of the crop for which the approximate value was given as $7,850, less 20 per cent commission charge of $1,570, plus transportation.

Again the vote was unanimous: accept the Barnfield offer.

One of the most troublesome questions still pending was: what to do with all the books in the front room of the library during the period of construction? If, as the architect said, the work might begin in April, a decision would have to be reached quite soon, and it would be no simple matter to pack the books, say in cartons, in such a way that whoever unpacked them could place them on the new shelves in correct alphabetical order with no loss of time. Furthermore, where could so very many cartons be stored for three months? One trustee proposed renting one of the vacant shops in the new Bradley Meadows Plaza; another volunteered to investigate the cost of hiring a trailer.

As a token of appreciation for her more than thirteen years of devoted work, the trustees held a small party for Lynn Wells at Deanie's in January of 1967. After a round of refreshments, Jane Laws read a poem entitled "A Life of Worth" by Richard F. Wolfe — a fitting description, she said, of Lynn's credo of service. Then Frances Rogers reminisced about earlier days, when Mrs. Wells first assumed her duties as librarian. As a parting gift the board presented her with a check for $100.

49

Frills and the Man from MHL

The more the Building Committee studied the architect's specifications, the more "frills" it found. "Why on earth hand-wrought nails for hand-wrought hinges for handmade shutters!" one of the members exclaimed. "And why a fancy ceiling of plywood and beams rather than a plain acoustical one? Has the man forgotten we have only $60,000 to spend?"

Before leaving for Florida, Fred Johnston, who remembered with pleasure a small library and its patio near his winter home in Key West, had said he hoped Mr. Milliken would include a patio in his design for the Woodstock Library. The architect did, of course, thus causing a split between the members of the Committee who regarded it as a charming idea and those who considered it an additional expense of questionable value in a northern climate. That was not the only bone of contention, however. A few of the members wanted a large basement under the new part — a room that could be used for community gatherings, musicales, or for the children, they said. Yet this would greatly add to the cost of construction.

The chairman, at her wit's end, decided to write to the State Library for advice. Enclosed with the reply from Albany were several manuals on library construction and while these were helpful they had little to say about basements and nothing at all about patios. So when the MHL (spurred on by the State Library) offered to send Mr. Roehr, a building consultant from the Mid-Hudson office, to Woodstock to meet with the Building Committee, the offer was promptly accepted.

Mr. Roehr, an expert in his field, proved to be a pleasant young man who listened attentively while the chairman briefed him on the background of the library's building plans, which included the $60,000 bequest, and the architect's efforts to keep everything as Colonial as possible. She also mentioned the specific points upon which the committee could not agree: the full basement and the patio, and then asked his opinion.

"Do not plan a large basement unless you have a particular use for it in mind," Mr. Roehr said. "Too often basement space is pressed into service for unsuitable use. In general a basement should not be used for shelving books."

That seemed to leave the door open; the committee would have to decide "what particular use" it had in mind. But there was no doubt whatever as to how Mr. Roehr felt about a patio. "Not recommended," he said flatly. "Expensive. And the policing would be a problem, both as to infringement of the law and litter." Nor did he approve of the architect's Colonial ceiling of plywood and beams. An acoustical ceiling was a must — either plaster or tile.

After studying the blueprints he said: "I see that these call for custom-made stacks but you would do far better to order standard library equipment. Standard size shelves are less expensive and are easier and cheaper to add to later."

One question the committee had been puzzling over was the arrangement of the rows of stacks in the new room and this, too, Mr. Roehr was equipped to answer. He had brought with him what he called a "Plan-o-matic" — a miniature set of library furnishings and a floor board with scale markings. By shifting the toy-like librarian's desk, the card catalog, tables, chairs, and rows of stacks about, one could discover how best to arrange them in relation to each other. The decision reached that day was carried out without change: the desk at the left of the entrance with the card catalog conveniently near, the chairs and tables on the opposite side of the room, and the rows of stacks lined up in the remaining space.

Progress was indeed being made. Even so, all thought of beginning construction before May had been dismissed. Too many problems lay ahead and only one of them was partly solved. The Junior Chamber of Commerce had offered to remove the books from the front room, an exacting job, but where they could be stored was another question.

When it became known that Mrs. Wells was retiring and no announcement had been made concerning a replacement (Mrs. Roberts had not as yet reached a decision), the trustees received a few applications from would-be librarians. As it turned out, however, most of the candidates interviewed were quite young and completely lacking in executive experience. Only one seemed even worthy of consideration, but she was not a college graduate, nor had she ever received instruction in library science. Her only qualification was that she had worked for quite a long time in a much larger library.

By contrast, Ellin Roberts, a Vassar graduate who had majored in English literature, and who was now prepared to take a course in library science, stood head and shoulders above the others. So, following her interview with the Board on March 18, 1967, the secretary was directed to write a letter offering her the position of head librarian as of Tuesday, January 2, 1968.

When Mrs. Wells had left in February, the Building Committee was still discussing changes in the architect's plans and it was anybody's guess when they could be put out for bids and the work get under way. The board, determined to keep the library open to the public as long as possible, asked the two assistant librarians if they would be willing to carry on, putting in extra hours in order to keep up with the work

load. Fortunately the two — Mrs. Charlotte Heller who had
been Mrs. Wells's assistant since September 1963, and Mrs.
Connie Catalano who had been with the library almost as
long — were willing to accept the responsibility.

The members of the Building Committee who wanted a
large waterproof basement suitable for community meetings
continued to argue for it even after the architect warned that
it might add $4,000, at least, to the cost of the building. Nor
were they willing to forego the patio. Finally, much to everyone's satisfaction, Mr. Milliken said he would ask contractors
for alternate bids: one for a large basement, the other for a
furnace room only, with crawl space. He would also ask for
a separate estimate on the patio.

When George Laws had examined the layout of the heating system as shown in the blueprints, he had been quick to
spot its weak points: right angles in the ducts, the need for
a furnace with a larger ETU, inadequate registers for both
outlet and intake. He had then volunteered to donate a design he himself would make which, for example, would include a humidifier to keep the books from becoming too dry
and a separate thermostat for the second-story room.

The chairman of the Committee had asked a lighting engineer from Central Hudson to review the proposed lighting
plans. After a careful check of the existing system, he advised new lighting for the office area and more fixtures in
stated places.

After George Laws had completed the drawings for his
proposed heating system, at his request an expert from Crane
in New York City made a special trip to Woodstock (donating his services) to judge the design. After stating that he
considered the "plan is a good heating layout," he made a
few suggestions. And as soon as George Laws had carried
them out, Mr. Milliken said that the way was now clear for
receiving bids. However, because of the complicated figuring

necessary in this case, it might be a month before all seven contractors being asked to place bids were ready to submit them. Therefore construction could not start before the first of July at the earliest.

The entry in the minutes reads: "Considerable discussion revolved around our problem of having a Fair with construction in progress . . . we are fairly certain that we will not have the grounds available on the east side due to the building but we may have the back and west side. . . . The estimate from Bro-Dart for shelves, card catalog and other things has been received: $4692 plus $430 for delivery and installation."

50

A Financial Jolt; An Endowment Plan; The Low Bid

On May 25, 1967, when everything seemed to be going so well, it was both a surprise and a shock to learn that the library must return $8,352.52 from its $60,000 Marsh bequest. Mr. Moscowitz informed the board that the lawyer for the estate and the executors had made a mistake in figuring the library's 15 per cent share. Since it had no choice in the matter, the board directed the Treasurer to write the necessary check. This left exactly $51,647.48 to cover all costs: construction, the architect's ten per cent fee, and Bro-Dart's bill.

When Louise Lindin suggested that the money from the Ives estate be used to cover the building costs, Carolyn Wilson said: "We are hoping to keep what we get from the sale of the Ives effects as the beginning of an endowment fund."

She had spoken about this at an earlier meeting, proposing a long-range plan: the establishment of an endowment for the library with the intention of eventually having a sum large enough so that the interest from it would "cover our annual operating expenses and therefore relieve the pressure on the Fair." Such an endowment, given the right publicity, she pointed out, "might cause others, as did Mrs. Marsh and Mrs. Ives, to leave the library important bequests." The entry in the minutes that day reads: "It was moved and unanimously passed that the $30,000 from the sale of the Ives furnishings be the beginning of such an endowment."

What the trustees were not aware of that day was that a resolution passed by one Executive Committee may be cancelled by a subsequent one. Legally an institution, such as the library, is bound to use a bequest for a specific purpose only if so stated in the will. Nevertheless, because no board since that vote was passed in 1967 has ever rescinded it, it is still in force and the $30,000 is indeed "the beginning of such endowment" — at least until it is annulled at some future date.

Another entry in the minutes of that same meeting states that a check for $1,000 had been received from the estate of the late Blanche Rosett. This time the trustees had not been asked if the library was incorporated, but since the question had been put to them more than once in the past, they now decided to get an official answer. A letter to the State Library in Albany brought a prompt answer: "In wills or legal documents the organization should be referred to as 'Woodstock Library, Woodstock, N.Y., a corporation chartered by the Board of Regents under the State Education Law.'"

In June of 1967 the following slate was elected: president, John Stefano; vice-president, Carolyn Wilson; treasurer, Ken Osterhoudt; secretary, Sharon Csonka. Retiring President Anita Goldberg read her report which began:

"This year has been a very eventful, busy and nerve-wracking year for the Library. Our activities were concentrated in two main areas. The first was the difficult task of finding a librarian to take Lynn Wells's place — this involved much thought, time and discussion. The Board is happy to report that it has signed a one-year contract with Mrs. Ellin Roberts, who is taking the required library course at Pratt, and who will begin her services with our Library on January 2, 1968. She is charming and competent and we are sure the appointment will be to Woodstock's advantage.

"The second event involves the new building and I cannot tell you how much energy, blood, sweat, and tears have gone into this project. I also cannot tell you how much Frances Rogers has contributed — she has been the driving force, the dynamo, the guardian of our interests. She has worked countless hours and has worried countless nights over plans and arrangements, interviews with the architect, with lighting and heating engineers, with library equipment, and we all owe her a tremendous vote of thanks. I would at this time request the Secretary to insert in the minutes our appreciation of sincere thanks on the part of the Board to Frances Rogers for her efforts. . . . Our new Library will cost a great deal more to run in maintenance, lighting, etc. and we still must make our Fair a success if we are to meet our budget. . . ."

On the morning of June 20, in response to a telephone call from Mr. Milliken, Miss Rogers was seated by the architect's desk in Kingston in order to be present while he opened the seven bids. She waited uneasily while he slit open the long envelopes and removed the standard forms, arranging them side by side before him. After what seemed a very long interval he exclaimed, "This is almost unbelievable! The top bid is from J. H. Schoonmaker and Sons — they are asking $70,691, less $2,044 if no patio, and an additional $5,709 for a full basement. And by contrast, the lowest figure, from the Schneider Brothers of New Paltz is $48,643, less $1,384 if no patio, and an additional $2,686 for a large basement. That's more than $22,000 difference on the basic bids! The Schneiders have made a mistake — omitted something. I'll call them now and check."

Miss Rogers, aware that the library now had only $51,647.48 to cover all expenses had, prior to this meeting, with Mr. Moscowitz's help, succeeded in obtaining papers exempting the library from the State Sales Tax, now sat with crossed fingers while Mr. Milliken carried on a lengthy conversation, his side of it consisting largely of questions. Then, turning to her, he said, "Stanley Schneider insists that their figures are correct, that they have omitted nothing and will stand behind their bid. The reason they can keep their bids low, he says, is because the firm is a family affair. They do all their own carpentry, plumbing, wiring and masonry and do not have to farm out anything to sub-contractors, which saves them quite a lot. They've recently completed a church, an addition to a library, and an apartment house in New Paltz and I think you'd be wise to consider them."

Here was wonderful news for the committee. The chairman called a meeting the following day — and ran straight into a snag. "How can we be sure they cut no corners to keep the cost down? Shoddy workmanship. Low quality materials. Even if the next bid is $7000 higher shouldn't we pay the difference so as to use a local man?"

Several meetings later the committee asked three of the trustees to make an appointment with the Schneiders, drive to New Paltz, inspect the church and other places, and size up the men themselves.

On the morning of July 6, Carolyn Wilson, Frances Rogers, and Vern May drove to New Paltz where they found young Stanley Schneider in work clothes on a construction job. He was forthright, sincere, and likeable. With obvious pride he pointed out the by-no-means-small apartment house, took them through the library, and showed them the stone church. As far as the three could judge, the Schneider Brothers' standards were high, their work expert.

At the trustees' meeting, held that same evening, the three who had made the trip to New Paltz recommended awarding the contract to the Schneider Brothers. After some discussion "it was moved by John Natoli to accept base bid by Schneider Bros. of $47,264 with certain deletions approved at subsequent Executive Meetings, to build Library addition. It was moved by Anthony Robinson to eliminate the plans for the basement. This motion was seconded by Mari Bollman and unanimously approved. It was moved by Mike Boyle to eliminate the terrace [the patio] from the plans. This motion was seconded by Frances Rogers and unanimously approved. . . ."

51

Letters to the Press; Construction Under Way

By this time a plan had been worked out for storing the many cartons of books: some would go on the floor of the children's room, the rest on the floor of the wing, thus distributing the weight. Gerge Laws had warned that since men would be working under both floors, there must be no risk of their giving way.

A news story, explaining why the Woodstock Library would be closed until the end of the year was released to the press and a week later, on July 20, the following letter appeared in the Woodstock *Week*.

Dear Library:

I think that it was unfair of you to close for so long a time. I had planned to take out a lot of books and now I have to buy any books I read over this summer.

I would not be so disappointed if you only closed for a small amount of time. In Princeton, my home town, the library which is three times as large took only two weeks and they moved into a new building.

Anyway, I am very disappointed and I am not going to the Library Fair as a result.

Chris Mark — *Age 11*
Wittenberg Road
Bearsville, N.Y.

The letter which began "Dear Chris" and appeared in the adjoining column was written by Vice-President Wilson with her usual charm. Here is an excerpt:

Let me tell you a little about the reasons for being closed. First is the fact that our Library building was originally built so many years ago that it sags and leaks and really needs repair. Second, and very important, a friend of the Library, like you, but many years older, gave us a lot of money so we could remodel the building. Her name was Mabel Marsh and she especially wanted to help the Library without changing it too much. If we built a brand new building and moved our books into it I think we might be able to do it as quickly as in your home town. However, we have to move the books out and store them while the renovation is going on and then move them back again. And the builders tell us it will take four months for them and as several builders agreed that is how long it would take, we cannot change that. I think you might be interested to come occasionally through the summer and watch the process of tearing down the old section and rebuilding a bigger and stronger building. . . ."

Like as not Chris changed his mind and did go to the Fair.

Under the skillful direction of Co-Chairmen Elizabeth Clough and Adele Longendyke, the Fair, held on the last Thursday in July, netted $7171. The following Monday the first of many truckloads of construction material arrived at the building site. Then on August 7 the noisy wrecking of the old building was in full swing amid clouds of dust.

As the long handhewn beams were wrenched from the ceiling they were stacked out front in the hope that they could be sold for re-use. They did attract considerable attention, but in the opinion of bargain seekers the asking price of $25 a beam was too high. Eventually a few of the better beams were sold and in February we find this brief entry in the minutes and not a word more: "Sale of beams $50."

Salvaged also were the two wooden posts on the small front porch and the mantlepiece from over the fireplace to be turned over to the Historical Society for its collection of Americana.

After the rubble had been cleared away and the old beams

under the office floor examined for dry rot, they were found to be in such a bad state of decay that the wonder of it was the floor boards had not sagged. Not only the underpinning but the whole wall between the office, the children's room, and the new part had to be replaced — an unforeseen expense not covered by the contract. That was the first of a number of extras for which the library had to foot the bill. The second followed close on its heels.

During excavation an underground spring was uncovered and since there was no way of stopping the endless flow of water, a sump pump and a drainpine would have to be installed, but the cost would not be excessive *if* the library were allowed to tap the large pipe crossing its property in front. Years earlier, when the trustees had wanted to tie in with the pipe in order to drain the parking area, Mr. Lasher had refused because, he said, the muddy water might clog the culvert. The spring water would carry no mud, however — a point to be stressed. Furthermore, now that Mr. Lasher and his wife were living in their new home opposite the post office and the house next door was occupied by the new funeral director, Robert Boyd, he was the one to approach.

On the morning that Frances Rogers and Carolyn Wilson set out on this quest they found Mr. Boyd at work in his flower garden. No one could have been more cooperative. He not only granted permission but also offered to put it in writing. But this seemed unnecessary — it was a gentleman's agreement.

Because of the many cartons stored on the floor of the wing, the trustees had to find other quarters in which to hold their meetings. For want of a larger place they accepted the town's offer of the sheriff's office, a room never free from the odor of stale tobacco. The Book Committee fared better. At the invitation of Lynn Wells the October meeting was held on the wide veranda of her home; the following month at Doris Lee's (that day there was no let-up on the rain), and in December at the Wilsons'.

When the trustees met in the sheriff's office in mid-September, work on the new building had not progressed much beyond a great hole in the ground — or so it seemed. But when the chairman of the Building Committee had questioned Stanley Schneider about being on schedule he had said: "We are. This part — the excavation and cellar — is the hard part. The framework will go faster." Since being on schedule meant having the work completed "on or about December 1," the trustees, in a spirit of anticipation, proceeded to make a list of guests to be invited to the official opening of the library, set, tentatively, for January 4 of the new year.

"As part of the festivities tea or punch in the new building was also discussed," Secretary Csonka wrote. "John Stefano will ask Ginger Anderson to be in charge of party arrangements."

Before the meeting adjourned the trustees had agreed upon a plan to launch a fund raising drive "to coincide with the opening of the new Library. The goal would be $100,000. . . ." There was no lack of enthusiasm; a committee of five was appointed to work out the details. Yet the following month it "was moved to endorse the concept of the fund drive but to table it for the time being."

Meanwhile, work on the new building was proceeding well and the trustees were impressed with the efficiency of the Schneiders and their crew. No group of men could have been more responsible or more pleasant to deal with. On November 14, during a tour of inspection, the Building Committee mounted the stairs for a look at the fine new room on the second floor and were impressed by its size.

The cornerstone from Woodstock, England, which had been laid with pomp and ceremony in 1948, had been carefully removed from the old wall of the wing. Completely forgotten, however, were the things that had been placed in the hollow section of the concrete block upon which it rested. But even if they had been rescued there would have been no place for them in the solid stones of the new foundation. In fact, there was scant room in the masonry for the corner-stone where it was relocated near the southeast corner of the new building.

52

Despite Delays, a "New" Library

If the Schneiders had not been called upon to do far more than originally planned, if the huge rolls of linoleum had been delivered on time, if several sections of stacks from Bro-Dart had not been accidentally omitted from the shipment, probably the work at the library would have been completed on schedule. By Friday, December 8, however, the linoleum was down and the four rows of double-faced stacks in place. The following Sunday the Jaycees, true to their word, arrived at one o'clock to begin the long arduous task of unpacking the many cartons of books. Under the supervision of Caroline Wilson and Ellin Roberts, and with the help of Connie and Charlotte, the fiction was lined up in the correct alphabetical order — an exacting job that left everyone bone tired.

The bronze plaque in memory of Walter Weyl that had been on the front of the old Library since 1927 was now inside on the west wall of the vestibule and below it was a matching plaque bearing the words:

IN MEMORY
OF
MABLE VAN ALSTYNE MARSH
WHOSE BEQUEST MADE POSSIBLE
THIS ADDITION TO THE LIBRARY
1967

A check for $100, contributed by Mrs. Alexander Archipenko, had covered the cost of the humidifier installed to prevent the books from becoming too dry during the winter months when the furnace was running. This was much appreciated by the trustees.

Not until all the statements were in was it learned how well the library had made out. Here, in brief, is the final accounting:

Basic contract (after deductions)		$46,404.00
Architect's fee 10%		4,640.40
		51,044.40
Additional costs not subject to fee:		
Schneider Brothers	$2,138.00	
Bro-Dart	5,122.00	
	7,260.00	7,260.00
	Total	$58,304.40
Revised Marsh bequest		51,647.48
	Deficit	$ 6,656.92

A small deficit indeed, all things considered, and it did not make too great a dent in the Library's savings account.

Tuesday, January 16, 1968, the first day the library reopened, many people ventured out in spite of the cold miserable weather. Sheer ice underfoot made walking risky and sent cars skidding. This was the public's first opportunity to see the interior of the new part of the building, and it was well worth a special trip. Ellin Roberts and her two capable assistants were very much on the job, prepared to check out books and accept membership dues.

The reception to celebrate the formal opening of the library was held on Sunday February 11, from three to six. It was a well-attended, gay party and the New Library, as some called it, looked both festive and ready for business. Readier than ever, in fact, with its greater space, handsome new shelving, tables and chairs, and much improved lighting. But, as always, with change and growth comes challenge, and behind the scenes there remained much to do if the library's services were to match its expanded and enhanced physical plant. It was indeed an occasion for celebration of great accomplishment and also — as those who had long been intimately involved with the library realized — for renewed dedication to its welfare and service for the future.

Today the future appears bright — there's a sense of continuity, of capacity for growth. True, much has been accomplished. What began as a horse-and-buggy village has burgeoned into a town with a population of over 5000. And with the development of nearby ski areas, the tourist season is no longer limited to the summer months. The presence of an IBM plant in nearby Kingston has brought families unfamiliar with Woodstock's history. Readers accustomed to fully tax-supported libraries expect service akin to their previous experience in much larger communities. The almost incredibly rapid expansion of the State University at New Paltz and the establishment of the Ulster Community College at Stone Ridge — all within easy commuting distance — have introduced new demands on the Woodstock Library for technical, academic resources to meet the needs of students and faculty at all levels. Moreover, within the past five years, there's been an influx of young people. Although the famous Woodstock Festival actually took place some sixty miles away, Woodstock has become something of a Mecca for the young. And they have brought with them their concerns with ecology, with crafts, with the search for a freshly meaningful way of life.

Change and growth are in the air. As the Woodstock Library reaches its sixtieth anniversary there are many plans afoot for increased services. The staff has doubled; circulation figures have mounted: more books checked out, more returned to the shelves; and library hours have been extended. Operating expenses have zoomed. The library's strength — its future — hinge on the will of the community to support it, and most particularly, as always, on the unflagging endeavor of dedicated men and women who are concerned with maintaining the unique and excellent qualities of the Woodstock Library.

Index